PAUL TEMP[LE]
THE CURZ[ON]

Francis Henry Durbridge was born in Hull, Yorkshire, in 1912 and was educated at Bradford Grammar School. He was encouraged at an early age to write by his English teacher and went on to read English at Birmingham University. At the age of twenty one he sold a play to the BBC and continued to write following his graduation whilst working as a stockbroker's clerk.

In 1938, he created the character Paul Temple, a crime novelist and detective. Many others followed and they were hugely successful until the last of the series was completed in 1968. In 1969, the Paul Temple series was adapted for television and four of the adventures prior to this, had been adapted for cinema, albeit with less success than radio and TV. Francis Durbridge also wrote for the stage and continued doing so up until 1991, when *Sweet Revenge* was completed. Additionally, he wrote over twenty other well received novels, most of which were on the general subject of crime. The last, *Fatal Encounter*, was published after his death in 1998.

Also in this series

FRANCIS DURBRIDGE

Paul Temple and the
Curzon Case

COLLINS
CRIME
CLUB

COLLINS CRIME CLUB

An imprint of HarperCollins*Publishers*
1 London Bridge Street
London SE1 9GF
www.harpercollins.co.uk

This paperback edition 2015

First published in Great Britain by
Coronet 1972

A catalogue record for this book is
available from the British Library

ISBN 978-0-00-812574-5

Set in Sabon by Born Group using Atomik ePublisher from Easypress

Printed and bound in Great Britain

MIX
Paper from
responsible sources
FSC
www.fsc.org   FSC™ C007454

Prologue

Dulworth Bay was a noisy place at night when the tide came in. The sea broke angrily against the shore, retreated with a rush of sand and pebbles and then crashed forward again. Ridges of white foam caught the moonlight as they rode towards the beach. The darkness was like a soundproof blanket pierced by a few stars and the distant lighthouse. The rowing boat a hundred yards out from the shore was alone, cut off by the noise.

A man rested on his oars and looked blindly into the sky; among the sounds of the sea he could distinguish the approaching drone of a twin-engined Hawker Siddeley; his eyes traced a path towards the coast as the aeroplane passed overhead. The man flashed a lamp three times in signal.

The drone of the engines grew louder again as the aeroplane circled back. Then the man saw a winking orange wing light passing through the clouds, dropping low out of the sky and swinging towards the cliffs. He didn't see the aircraft until the roar of the engines became a screech of agony several seconds later. He heard a dull explosion, and simultaneously a lick of white light shot into the sky. Fire billowed down the cliffs and burned itself out in the sea.

1

The man in the boat watched for nearly a minute, and then quite slowly he pulled towards the wreckage.

Chapter One

'Here's to crime,' Scott Reed said benevolently, raising his glass in a toast to the manifestly law-abiding company. 'And long may it prosper.'

Paul Temple looked from his publisher to the circle of guests with drinks in their hands. 'One eminent French criminologist has argued that there are no crimes, there are only criminals.'

'That was Professor Saleilles,' said Steve Temple deflatingly. She turned to Scott Reed. 'Don't worry, Scott. The French professor was much less scientific than your Dr Stern. He hadn't done experiments with rats.'

The publisher looked startled. 'I'm pleased to hear it.' He glanced over his shoulder at the man whose book on crime was the excuse for the party. 'Did Dr Stern do experiments with rats?'

'Of course,' said Steve. 'He describes them in detail.' She laughed teasingly. 'I thought you always read the books you publish?'

Scott Reed sighed. 'I don't always understand them.'

Dr Albert Stern was not looking the part of a literary lion. He stood in the corner of the room watching the throng of journalists, criminologists and novelists with the apprehension of a man caught in lewd company. There was a clutch of thriller writers discussing their overseas sales, two policemen looking as if they were guarding the drink, and an assistant commissioner from Scotland Yard was sitting on the sofa reading *The Psychology of Crime*. Dr Stern had been told to chat up the booksellers, but the booksellers all seemed to know each other and they preferred to talk among themselves.

'Do rats,' Scott Reed asked after careful thought, 'steal from each other and murder their wives?'

'Only when they come from bad homes,' said Steve.

She glanced at herself in the ornately carved mirror above the imitation Adam fireplace. She was wearing a sheer maxi dress with varying degrees of subtle see-through, printed in bands of colour that ranged through blues, reds and mauves. Captivating, Steve thought to herself. So much more restrained than the vulgarly fashionable girl Scott Reed employed as his publicity officer.

Steve half listened to somebody arguing that capital punishment gave added zest to a murder mystery, while her husband's group discussed crime in general. She took a dry martini from a passing tray. As the only person in the room who had read the doctor's book Steve felt a certain aloofness towards the gossip. She felt that Paul was being obtuse about it.

'How can you write a book on the psychology of crime?' he had asked three times on the way to the party. 'There are so many different types of crime. I mean, you could write about delinquency or the aggressive impulse—'

'He does,' Steve had said patiently.

'Criminals are not personality types,' Paul had continued. 'They're people who've committed a crime, that's all, by sudden temper or under provocation, under stress. Unless they're psychopaths.'

'That's what he says,' Steve had murmured.

'Absurd!'

An elderly lady novelist was bearing down upon Steve with a flourish of her stole and the glint of a storyteller in her eye. Steve turned quickly to the police inspector standing beside her. 'I didn't realise crime was so dull,' she said. 'I don't think you're going to make many arrests this evening.'

Inspector Vosper was hurt. 'I'm here in my private capacity,' he protested. 'Mr Temple said I should masquerade as a human being for one evening.'

'What happens when the clock strikes midnight?' Steve asked him.

Charlie Vosper looked every inch a policeman with his blue shirt and black tie, plain clothes and cropped grey hair. 'I turn back into a pumpkin.' He prodded a finger confidentially into Steve's left arm. 'What do you think of this psychology nonsense, eh? How many burglars do you suppose Dr Stein has caught red-handed?'

'Dr Stern,' she corrected him. 'I don't suppose he—'

'Exactly. Would he recognise an embezzler if he stood next to one in a bank? Unless he was wearing a mask!'

'He explains in his book—'

'Books are all very well, Mrs Temple,' the inspector said heavily. 'But a policeman's job is ninety per cent routine hard work and ten per cent knowing the criminal and pinning the rap on him. Dr Stein can't teach me how to apprehend a murderer.'

'That's what he says,' Steve murmured. 'Dr Stern.'

'Ridiculous!'

Steve sat wearily on the sofa by the assistant commissioner. 'What do you make of it, Sir Graham?' she asked. 'Are you wishing Paul hadn't dragged you along to this party?'

'Not really, although the place is rather short on pretty girls. Only one attractive female in sight.' Sir Graham Forbes closed the book and looked about the room. He was a dapper man with a bouncy, military manner, a military moustache and the steel blue eyes of a soldier. 'The trouble with crime is that it doesn't give the women a chance. Look at Paul over there, discussing penal reform with all those dreary men. He's neglecting his wife.'

'Bless you,' said Steve, giving him a kiss on his bristling cheek.

The criticism was not altogether warranted. Paul was at the drinks table jostling among the journalists to get his glass refilled. He emerged eventually from the scrum and tottered across to the sofa.

'Hello,' said Paul. 'You look like an oasis of sanity in this mad publishing world. Can I join you?' He sat on the floor beside the sofa. 'Oh dear. Crime is too serious a matter to be left to experts. Have you ever heard so much nonsense talked?'

'Sir Graham,' Steve explained, 'has been regretting the absence of women from the ranks of crime. Down with male domination, that's what we say.'

Paul laughed. 'I'll drink to that. Dr Stern forgot to mention sexual differences, didn't he?' He looked triumphantly at Steve. 'I knew the book wasn't thorough! And poor old Scott is beginning to wish he'd never published it. He's threatening to sack his non-fiction editor for committing the firm to a book about rats.'

'Rats?' Inspector Vosper repeated nervously.

'Yes, Scott is losing his grip. He assumed that because there were graphs and footnotes it was a scholarly work.'

'Paul,' said his wife disloyally to the others, 'is another of those people who think that psychology is bunk.'

'That's not true! But I am an arts man, and I think that detection is something to do with logic and understanding people, having intuition and predicting individual behaviour.'

'Hard work and attention to detail,' Inspector Vosper muttered audibly.

'Detection?' said Sir Graham. 'But the book isn't about detection, is it?'

'Of course not,' said Steve.

'Then what the devil are we doing here?' Paul demanded indignantly. 'Why did Scott ask me to bring along the cream of the British police force? I thought it was a handy manual on spotting crooks by the bumps on their heads. I wouldn't have agreed to review it if I'd known.'

'I suppose,' the assistant commissioner said thoughtfully, 'that we detectives understand crime, understand the psychology of crime if you like. But we don't reach our understanding by experiments on rats, or by statistics. Charlie has understanding, but it's not the kind of thing that can be described in a book. For instance, Charlie was telling me this evening of a case that he's—'

Inspector Vosper coughed and straightened his shoulders.

'What's the matter?' Sir Graham demanded. 'I was going to tell Temple about those two boys—'

'Yes, sir, that's what I assumed. I wondered whether that would be discreet.'

'Discreet?' The military voice barked with exasperation. 'Discretion is for inspectors, man! An assistant commissioner can be as indiscreet as he likes!'

'Yes, sir.'

'If we were discreet we'd accept that no crime had been committed and get on with our work.'

'Yes, sir.'

'And don't keep on saying yes, sir, like that. This is an informal occasion. Relax and look as though you're enjoying the art of conversation. Sit down, man.'

'Yes, sir.' Vosper sat on a stiff-backed chair and tried to compose his stern features into a relaxed order. He was doing quite well until Steve began choking with laughter.

'The point is that no crime has been committed,' Sir Graham resumed. 'At least, not that we know of. We've simply had a missing persons report, and that wouldn't justify a full scale investigation. But Vosper thinks the situation should be looked into, and he's usually right about these matters. A first class detective has a nose for anything not quite right.'

'Really?' said Paul with bland innocence. 'Intuition, eh?'

'What I call nose-ology,' said Sir Graham. 'But I looked it up in the index of Dr Stern's book and he doesn't mention it.'

'Tell me,' said Paul, 'about these two missing boys.'

Vosper glanced at the assistant commissioner, then cleared his throat. 'Do you know Dulworth Bay?' he asked conversationally.

'It's a fishing village in Yorkshire,' said Paul. 'A beautiful spot. We know it well.'

'Ah, so you probably know St Gilbert's. It's a minor public school. Quite a good one, so I'm told. They have a hundred boarders and fifty day boys. The headmaster is a Reverend Dudley Clarke.'

Steve found that her attention was straying. Charlie Vosper lacked the eye for detail which makes for a good raconteur. 'I suppose,' she said flippantly, 'that Young Woodley has run off with the housemaster's wife?'

'I don't think so,' said Vosper. 'Who is Woodley?'

'The missing boys are called Baxter,' said the assistant commissioner. 'They live with their father in a cottage on the Westerby estate. Their mother died about two years ago. Carry on, Charlie, tell them what happened.'

Vosper signalled to the publicity girl for another drink before he continued. He was a beer drinking man himself, but he was apparently reconciled to the rules being changed for one evening. He sipped a large whisky.

'Three weeks ago last Tuesday,' said Vosper, 'Michael and Roger Baxter and another boy left St Gilbert's after school and walked the mile or so to the Baxter cottage together. When they reached the cottage Michael Baxter remembered that he'd left a book at the school. It was a book he needed for prep that evening so he went back to fetch it. Left his brother and the other lad sitting on a fence in front of the cottage.'

He took another sip at the whisky. 'Well, to cut a long story short, those two boys waited for nearly an hour, and then Roger Baxter decided to go back to school and look for his brother. The other boy went home. At seven o'clock that evening Mr Baxter, the father, became worried about the boys and went to the school. You can guess the story. The headmaster hadn't seen the Baxter boys, they hadn't gone back to the school, and they haven't been seen since.'

'I guessed it,' said Paul. 'And how did they get on with their father?'

'Extremely well.' Vosper nodded emphatically. 'There was obviously nothing premeditated about this business, Temple. That was the first thing that interested me. They were perfectly normal teenagers, plenty of friends in the village, they were good at sport, interested in girls. Michael is seventeen and he's particularly friendly with a Miss

9

Maxwell. She's a niece of Lord Westerby's and lives at the Hall.'

'Diana Maxwell?' asked Paul.

'Yes. I thought you might have heard of her. She writes poetry, although you wouldn't think so to meet her. She looks quite normal.'

'Charlie popped up to Dulworth Bay,' explained the assistant commissioner, 'semi-officially. The local inspector invited him up for a couple of days. That was when nose-ology came into the case. Charlie found that his nostrils were twitching.'

'There may be nothing to it,' said Vosper modestly. There was only one peculiar detail I could point to, and that may not be significant. But the Baxter boys share a bedroom; it's a large, pleasant room, more like a playroom in some ways, and it overlooks the lane. I searched it, of course, read through the exercise books and the adolescent stuff that you'd expect to see. But the interesting oddity was a cricket bat.'

'A boy's proudest possession,' said Paul Temple. 'I remember how I kept mine oiled and supple—'

'That's the picture,' said Charlie Vosper. 'Young Roger Baxter is fourteen, and he'd collected the autographs of the St Gilbert's first eleven on the blade of his bat. Struck me as a funny thing to do, but at my school we used cricket bats to hit each other with when we used them at all. So I made a check on the names, and there was one which I couldn't account for.' He smiled, pleased with himself. 'It wasn't even a genuine signature. Roger Baxter had written it there himself.'

'What was the name?' asked Paul.

'The name,' pronounced Inspector Vosper, 'was Curzon.'

'Just Curzon? No Christian name or initials?'

'Just Curzon!' Vosper placed his empty glass on a nearby table and watched it in the hope that it might be miraculously refilled. But it was every man for himself now and the journalists had the drink pinned at the far end of the room. 'I wouldn't claim that the name has any particular significance,' he said. 'Only that it was odd. I was looking for oddities by that time.'

'You see, Temple,' the assistant commissioner interrupted, 'that's nose-ology. Nobody at the school has heard of anyone called Curzon. Charlie asked the boys' father and the name was completely unknown to him. Unknown to everyone else in Dulworth Bay. So what made Roger Baxter write it on his precious cricket bat?'

'Charlie has a nose for detail,' murmured Paul. 'I wonder what Dr Stern would make of the story?'

Steve sighed and rose to her feet. 'I know, don't say it: his book is ridiculous.'

'Nonsense,' agreed Sir Graham.

'Paul, are we going home? I'm tired and the noise in this room is giving me a headache. I can scarcely see who's doing the shouting through this cigarette smoke. I need some fresh air.'

It was a quarter to ten. Paul took her arm and went in search of Scott Reed.

'I'm fed up with cocktail parties!' said Scott, staring at a burn and three whisky stains on the carpet. 'I do hope it hasn't been too boring, Temple. Goodbye, Steve, so good of you to have kept those detectives amused.'

Kate Balfour had long since gone home, so Paul pottered about in the kitchen producing the cocoa. He prided himself on his masculine independence. He could make cocoa without burning the milk and boil an egg without the yolk becoming

11

solid. He took the drinks upstairs to the living room flushed with a sense of achievement.

'I hope we didn't leave too abruptly,' he said as he put the tray on the table. 'You didn't even tell Dr Stern how much you admire his book.'

'I didn't admire it,' Steve confessed. 'But I did read the wretched thing, which is why I found the rest of you so irritating.' She went across to the telephone answering machine on the shelf beside Paul's desk. The large room was furnished in two halves separated by a step. Paul's study was the half above the garage. 'We left abruptly because I didn't want you to start advising the police how to do their job. I know how they resent it—'

'I thought Sir Graham was inviting my opinion.'

'He may have been, but he's only the assistant commissioner. Charlie Vosper is the man who does the work, and he didn't want your advice. He'll make Sir Graham pay for tonight's little indiscretion, I could see it from his eyes.'

Steve smiled at the thought and absently pressed the button on the automatic answering machine. It whirred gently as the loop tape spun back to the beginning. 'This is Paul Temple's residence,' said the recorded voice. 'Mr and Mrs Temple are not available, but if you care to leave a message . . .'

Paul sank back into the armchair and drank his cocoa. He was beginning to hate the anonymous actor whose voice punctuated the messages; he always avoided switching on the machine until he was properly fortified against the day by three cups of coffee.

The telephone rang three times and the actor repeated his piece. 'Gor,' said a man in disgust, 'I'll write you a bloody letter.' The telephone clicked, rang three times, and the actor spoke again. It was nerve-racking.

'Damn,' said a girl's voice. 'Oh well, this is Diana Maxwell. I needed to speak urgently to Mr Temple. Tell him I'll ring him back, will you? I do hate all these mechanised gadgets!'

Paul rose to his feet in astonishment. 'What did she say her name was?'

'Exactly,' said Steve. 'Now isn't that a coincidence?' She spun the tape back to replay the message. 'She's the poet who seemed quite normal to Charlie Vosper.'

'It isn't a coincidence,' Diana Maxwell explained when she telephoned the next day. 'Inspector Vosper visited me on Friday and he mentioned your literary cocktail party. I think Westerby Hall brought out the democrat in him, but all his resentment was displaced on to your literary shindig. He said you would make him look like a penguin.'

'Charlie Vosper has always walked like that,' said Paul. 'Why did you want to talk to me?'

'I need your help, Mr Temple. Now that the police are searching for the Baxter brothers I think I'm in danger.'

'I'm a busy man, Miss Maxwell,' he said politely, 'and I never interfere in the work of the police. Inspector Vosper is specially trained to protect people in danger.' And the danger, Paul reflected, could not be imminent. She had waited three days to telephone him after the inspector's visit, and a further twenty-four hours had passed before she rang back. 'In danger from whom?' Paul asked.

'Someone by the name of Curzon.'

Paul walked round the desk and sat in his swivel chair. 'Go on, Miss Maxwell.' Full marks, he thought, to the inspector's nose. 'Tell me about Curzon.'

'Not over the telephone. Do you know the Three Boars in Greek Street? I'll meet you there at eight o'clock.' She clearly

13

did not expect any argument. 'I'll recognise you, but just for the record I'm wearing a blue suit, no hat; blue handbag. I'm fair, twenty-three and reasonably pretty.'

Paul smiled to himself. 'I had formed that impression, Miss Maxwell. You know what Robert Browning said: "The devil hath not in all his quiver's choice"—'

'An arrow for the heart like a sweet voice,' she completed. 'But for your information, Mr Temple, it was Lord Byron.'

They had to park nearly two hundred yards from the Three Boars. Paul took his wife's arm and walked through the neon-lit glitter of the Latin quarter. It lacked the vitality and charm, he reflected sadly, of the days when he had first got to know his London. The colour had been replaced by commercialism, it was no longer crime and vice for the simple pleasure of it. Or perhaps nostalgia was playing tricks with his memory.

'This shouldn't take us long,' said Paul. 'Where do you fancy eating afterwards?'

'Wheelers?' suggested Steve.

'Clever me,' murmured Paul. 'I've booked a table for nine o'clock.'

'Clever.'

The Three Boars was just another Soho pub, but the room upstairs was used for poetry readings and so the new literacy was centred on the bars. The barmaid with the flaxen hair and large bosom had been the inspiration of two sonnets, an ode to joy, and a somewhat clinical poem about sex. The clientele, Paul noticed as they went through to the saloon bar, looked conventional enough, except that the restrained young men in grey suits were probably known to the police, and the four scruffy characters shouting at each other in the corner were poets.

'Blue suit, twenty-three,' Paul said to himself. The girl by the door was pretty, but she didn't look like a poet. She looked rather different. She waved.

'I'm Diana Maxwell,' she gasped. 'It's awfully good of you to come like this. I do appreciate—'

Paul bought the drinks while Steve took care of the small talk. He watched the girl in the mirror behind the bar. A striking figure, elegantly dressed, but for a niece of Lord Westerby surprisingly lacking in poise. She fiddled with her long blonde hair as she talked and kept glancing about the room.

'Did anyone follow you here?' she asked when Paul arrived with the drinks. 'Did you notice a large red saloon car?'

'Don't worry,' said Paul. 'Parking is so bad in London now that gangsters travel by taxi.'

The girl tried to smile. 'I'm sorry, Mr Temple. I'm not used to physical danger. Six weeks ago I was leading a perfectly ordinary life. That's why I'm frightened. They've already tried to kill me twice, and sooner or later they'll succeed.'

'Now listen,' said Paul with a laugh, 'I know that two boys have vanished into thin air, but—'

'You don't know much about Curzon, do you?'

'That's true,' Paul agreed. 'That's why I'm here, remember? You telephoned me and said you'd been talking to Charlie Vosper. We quoted Byron at each other.' He broke off. Two men had come into the bar with that purposeful look of debt collectors in search of a defaulter. 'So tell me about Curzon, Miss Maxwell.'

'Of course,' she said quickly. 'It was good of you to come.' The two men moved together into the centre of the room. 'Five weeks ago when I was staying at Westerby Hall I came across—' The larger of the two men took a pistol from his raincoat pocket and fired it from point-blank range. The girl stared in dismay before spinning backwards off her chair. A sudden cavity appeared in the side of her neck and filled with blood.

'Get down, Steve, for God's sake!' Paul shouted.

The two men ran before the panic started. They were gone when Paul Temple reached the street. He caught a glimpse of a red saloon car driving away. People were screaming in the bar, several men spilled into the street, and when Paul returned he found a crowd staring down at the girl—

Steve was kneeling beside the girl's head, dabbing ineffectually at the wound with a Kleenex. She looked up at Paul. 'Diana Maxwell is dead,' she murmured.

Paul picked up a broken sherry glass from the carpet. A pool of blood had been seeping towards it. 'If this poor kid is dead,' he said in bewilderment, 'somebody has blundered. Because she is not Diana Maxwell.'

Chapter Two

Dulworth Bay had been a fishing village since Saxon times, and according to local legend it had then been a popular landing place for marauding Danes. The older families were still predominantly blonde-haired, and the growth of modern Britain had made little impact on their culture. The village was built precariously round the bay, ramshackle houses poised on the cliffs and steep winding streets plunging down to the beach.

A sprinkling of artists had moved into the village, and a few weekend people from Leeds and Middlesbrough had bought weekend houses, but they didn't belong. In Dulworth Bay you remained a foreigner for three generations, and holiday-makers were encouraged to keep moving until they reached Scarborough twenty miles to the south. To the west, a few hundred yards inland, the Whitby moors extended into nothing.

It was a remote spot, yet the police grapevine covered it effectively. A brief telephone call from Inspector Vosper to his north-country colleague ensured that Paul Temple's visit to Yorkshire was doomed to frustration.

'But this visit is nothing to do with your Baxter brothers,' Steve had protested innocently. 'This is a purely nostalgic holiday. I used to know Whitby years ago.'

'I don't,' the inspector had said doggedly, 'want you involved.'

Paul Temple had been slightly exasperated. 'When a girl asks for my help and is then killed sitting beside me, Charlie, I think I become involved. Whether you and I like it or not. I promised I'd help Miss Maxwell, because she was afraid—'

'Miss Maxwell is alive and well and staying in Yorkshire!' said Vosper. When they were out of earshot he telephoned Inspector Morgan. The mention of Assistant Commissioner Forbes had clinched it: they would treat Paul Temple and his wife with impeccable good manners and absolute inscrutability.

They were staying at the Victoria Hotel in Whitby, as a gesture towards diplomacy. It would look less, Paul had thought, as though they were investigating the Dulworth Bay mystery. But Inspector Morgan paid them a courtesy visit on the first morning after their arrival. 'Just to see whether I can be of help,' he said diplomatically. 'Mrs Temple may have forgotten her way around after all those years in the south . . .' Inspector Morgan was stationed in Whitby, which he clearly thought would be convenient for them all. 'Where were you thinking of visiting?'

Steve mentioned St Gilbert's, 'Although I think I can find it without having to trouble you, Inspector.'

'St Gilbert's?' he repeated inscrutably. 'I don't suppose you're telling me that Mrs Temple wants to visit her old school?' He seemed about to wink at Paul. 'Because St Gilbert's is a boys' school.' He stared smugly at Steve's trim figure.

'One of the masters is an old friend of my uncle's,' she explained. 'I haven't seen him since I was fourteen. He was the Latin master in those days, which is probably why I still find *amo-amas-amat* slightly romantic. I've invited him to dinner this evening.'

'Sounds as though it should be fun,' said the inspector. 'Have you planned many other trips down memory lane?'

'Westerby Hall?' Paul suggested.

'Westerby Hall,' the inspector repeated with impeccable good manners. 'Ah yes, that's where Lord Westerby lives.'

'Quite.'

'I don't,' he said cannily, 'know whether Miss Maxwell is staying with him at the moment.'

'Never mind,' said Paul. 'If she isn't there I'm sure the walk will have done us good. Our journey won't be wasted. There's nothing like the Yorkshire moors—'

'I did hear a rumour that Miss Maxwell is dead.'

'False, Inspector Morgan, as you well know!'

Paul Temple had tried to find Miss Maxwell in London, but she had proved elusive. The flat which she shared with a girl called Bobbie Jameson had been empty when he called. Miss Jameson was dead and Miss Maxwell had left for Yorkshire. Paul had let himself in the front door with a sliver of perspex against the lock, and he had spent nearly half an hour searching for something to indicate what the girls were mixed up with. But he found nothing.

It was obvious that Diana Maxwell used the flat merely as a *pied-a-terre* when she was in London. There were few possessions or papers belonging to her, and most of the photographs were of Bobbie Jameson. She had been the girl in the pub.

The instinct for self-preservation which had prompted Diana Maxwell to send a substitute had also led her straight back to Yorkshire when death had struck. But three hundred miles, Paul reflected sourly, was not very far if someone was determined to kill you.

Despite his boast to Inspector Morgan Paul drove out to Westerby Hall. He saw no reason to overdo the healthy life. The Yorkshire countryside was spectacular, but better appreciated from behind the wheel of a car. By foot it could reduce a man to exhaustion and madness. It made a man feel small. Westerby Hall was a mile inland from Dulworth Bay, nestling in a valley as if in hiding.

'Let's walk up to the house, darling,' Steve suggested as a compromise to physical fitness. 'We can look at these incredible wrought iron gates. I do believe they're by Tijou.'

They parked by the monumental gates. Steve examined them ecstatically, talking of Tijou's work at Hampton Court and speculating on the likelihood of the master travelling so far north.

There was a stream running along the high brown stone wall of the estate, and Paul's eyes followed the glittering band of water through the valley. He could hear a noise like angry wasps approaching, and then in the distance he noticed a tiny green sports car driving much too fast down the hill from the moors. Its wheels visibly left the road as it leaped across a hump backed bridge and the noise of the engine became a roar.

'Woman driver,' said Paul.

Steve had decided the gates were superb imitations. She turned away reluctantly to watch the sports car. 'She looks like a woman after your own heart,' said Steve ironically. 'Do you think someone's chasing her?'

'I wouldn't be at all surprised,' Paul said with a laugh.

She was doing at least seventy miles an hour along the narrow lane towards them. A girl's blonde hair streamed out behind her, reminding Paul of advertisements for motor oil. The aggressive thrust of the engine seemed to pause and the noise rose an octave as the girl changed gear.

'She's trying to stop,' Paul muttered.

'Brakes?' suggested Steve.

The car slithered suddenly, shuddered on to the grass verge, and without reducing speed travelled straight at Paul and Steve. It was almost entirely out of control, yet somehow the girl at the wheel managed to avoid them and smash into the wrought iron gates. The car came to rest several yards into the grounds with a tangle of irreplaceable metal twisted round the bonnet.

'Damn!' said the blonde.

She leapt miraculously from the wreckage and waved to Paul. 'Sorry if I startled you,' she called. 'The bloody brakes failed.' Her head disappeared beneath the front wheels while she tried to trace the mechanical fault.

'Those beautiful gates,' Steve said softly. 'Look at the mess. And she hit them on purpose, to avoid the wall.'

'And to avoid us,' said Paul as he ambled across to the car. 'I'm rather glad she doesn't know much about art.' He stared down at the girl's lime-green slacks.

She wriggled out from under the wheels as he watched. 'There you are,' she said irritably, 'the track rods have snapped in two.'

Paul gestured sadly at the buckled bonnet. 'I'm afraid that's a minor detail now, Miss Maxwell. You need a new engine, and the chassis looks none too healthy.' But he glanced under the wheels to see the offending brakes. 'Dangerous,' he murmured.

'I'll get my uncle to send the chauffeur down. He can at least have it towed away.' She stood up and turned to look at Paul with her full attention. An impressive girl with pale blue eyes, much more commanding and poised than the girl in the cafe. 'How do you know my name?' she asked.

'We've spoken to each other on the telephone,' said Paul. 'I recognise your voice. You rang me in London. My name's Temple, and the lady trying to mend the gates is my wife Steve.'

'Hello,' Steve called.

The girl was surprised. 'I've no idea what you mean,' she began. 'I don't know—'

'You asked me to meet you in the Three Boars,' said Paul. 'But it was very wise of you not to come. You might have been killed.' He smiled sympathetically. 'By the way, I'm terribly sorry about your friend Bobbie Jameson. She was a nice girl. Her death must have been a great shock to you.'

Her pale blue eyes were coldly deliberate. 'I didn't ask you to meet me, Mr Temple. I've never spoken to you on the telephone and I wish you hadn't told the police I had. It caused me some embarrassment.'

Paul shrugged and held open the door of his car. 'I'm sure my friend Inspector Vosper was the soul of tact. Can I give you a lift to the Hall? It's a long walk up this drive.'

She climbed into Paul's car without a word. Wilful, Paul decided, temperamental, like a well-bred race horse. He waited until Steve was safely in the car beside him and then drove off.

'It's my belief,' Paul resumed a few moments later, 'that you did speak to me on the telephone, Miss Maxwell, that you made the appointment and then changed your mind at the last minute. I suspect you gave poor Miss Jameson a pretty accurate briefing, and that her story about three attempts having been made to kill you was true.'

She tossed her head so that the long blonde hair bounced angrily on her shoulders. 'If I'd taken the trouble to make an appointment I should have kept it.'

The house was seventeenth century with early Victorian embellishments. It was much larger than it had appeared in the perspective of the valley. Paul drew up by the huge oak doors of the entrance. Almost immediately a young man came round the side of the house.

'Hello,' said the young man. 'Something wrong?'

'Yes,' said Diana Maxwell. 'I've smashed up the Aston Martin. Ran into those bloody gates. And to make matters worse this is Paul Temple and his wife.'

'Oh dear, the man who set the police on to you.' He turned with an amused expression to Paul. 'We heard you were up in Yorkshire, Mr Temple. I suppose you've come to apologise to Diana?'

'Not quite,' said Paul. 'I was really hoping for an explanation.'

'Diana never explains anything,' said the young man. 'She's much too aristocratic. Have you found the Baxter kids yet?'

His name was Peter Malo and his official role was secretary to Lord Westerby. But he behaved with proprietorial ease, helping Diana from the car and listening to her account of the crash at the entrance to the estate with humorous detachment.

'Never mind, you're alive and the car was insured,' he said as he led her away. 'And I've always thought those wrought iron monstrosities should be removed.' He turned back, as if he had suddenly remembered Paul's existence. 'By the way, Temple,' he called, 'Lord Westerby wondered whether you could have dinner the day after tomorrow? Half past eight?'

'We'll be delighted,' said Paul.

'Perhaps you'll have found the Baxter kids by then. Lord Westerby is worried about them, you know. Terribly worried.'

'Why?'

The young man was taken aback. 'Well, he is the squire, you know, he takes a benevolent interest in the community. Noblesse oblige.' He waved carelessly and led Diana Maxwell away round the side of the house. 'See you both the day after tomorrow.'

Paul Temple let in the clutch and drove away. It had been a frustrating afternoon so far. He wouldn't learn much from Diana Maxwell or the supercilious young man unless they chose that he should.

'What did you make of Miss Maxwell?' he asked Steve.

Steve looked at the wreckage of the sports car as they drove past the gates. 'A reckless driver,' she murmured.

'Not as reckless as all that,' said Paul. 'Her brake rods had been sawn nearly through with a hacksaw. They were bound to snap when she needed them most. Somebody tried to kill her, and I think she knew it.'

Paul drove in silence, up on to the moors and across the deserted wastes of green and purple heather. There was a strong breeze whistling over the undulating slopes which added to the sense of desolation. Sheep grazed unconcernedly at the roadside and far to the south the globes of the four minute warning system glinted in the sun.

'Are we going somewhere?' asked Steve.

'I thought we might have tea in Goathland. Do you remember the first time I came up here, just after we met?'

'Sentimental,' murmured Steve.

They had a pot of tea for two and toasted scones in the most remote spot in England. Years ago they had discussed whether the village was named after the goats who inhabited the moors or the Goths who might have found it congenial for battles. There was a church, a post office stores, and a few houses straggled along the roadside. It had seemed an idyllic retreat in those days, when walking twenty miles had been pleasurable and sleeping in a tent had been a sensuous treat.

'I think I'll have one of those cream pastries,' Steve said unromantically. 'And then we'd better hurry. Don't want to be late for our Latin school master. He's a devil for punctuality, and he'll have to get the boy back to the school before lights out.'

The schoolmaster was vague and affable; he talked about Steve's uncle with the uncertainty of a man who usually finds he is discussing the wrong boy with the wrong parents. His name was Elkington and he arrived early with a sixteen-year-old youth in a blue school cap.

'*Consul victor em laudat,*' Paul said affably.

'Very well, thank you,' said the Latin master. 'Have you met John Draper? He's the boy you asked—'

'*Militibus turpe est captivos male custodivisse.*'

Steve had to take Paul aside and explain that Mr Elkington was in fact English. 'He used to double up as the sports master. He scored a century the last time I saw him play.' So Paul discussed cricket with them over dinner, in English, which made conversation easier. It was one of the subjects which John Draper could discuss with authority.

The meal was English, with steaks and roast potatoes and garden peas, followed by apple pie. It was the only sort of meal to have in a northern hotel, Paul had felt, and he was enjoying the evening until the fair-haired youth exploded the pretence at polite conversation.

'Isn't it time you asked me the questions, Mr Temple?' he asked suddenly. 'I have to be back at school in two hours.'

'Really, Draper!' the Latin master protested. 'This is a purely social—'

'I've already told the police all I know about the Baxter brothers, so I'm afraid I shan't be much help.'

Paul grinned. 'You're quite right, John, I did ask Mr Elkington to bring you so that we could discuss the Baxter brothers. Why did you agree to come, I wonder?'

'I wanted to meet you, Mr Temple. I read some of your books when I was in the sanatorium and I thought they were rather good.' The slightly secretive smile was still hovering about the boy's mouth. 'And that police inspector said that on no account should I tell you anything, so I was thrilled to bits when the Elk said he was bringing me along. Er— I mean Mr Elkington.'

Mr Elkington coughed awkwardly. 'The boys call me the Elk,' he explained.

'I'm anti the police,' said the boy. 'I'm going to university next year.'

'The police appear to be anti me at the moment,' said Paul with a laugh. 'So suppose you tell me what you told the police? You went home with the Baxter brothers on the afternoon they disappeared, didn't you? It is possible that some apparently insignificant detail will prove to be important later. What happened when Roger went in search of his brother?'

The allegiances had been established, and the boy assumed a confidential manner. 'I went home. I popped into the Baxter cottage to tell their father I couldn't wait, and then I went home.'

'Did you walk home?'

'Yes, sir.'

'How far away do you live?'

'About a mile and a half. It's straight down the lane.'

'Did you see anyone in the lane?'

'No, sir.'

'Did you hear anything?'

The boy's self-confidence faltered. 'No,' he said after a pause. 'I don't think so. What sort of thing do you mean?'

He looked nervously at the Elk. 'Do you mean anything suspicious?'

'Anything at all,' murmured Paul.

'I don't think I heard anything.'

Paul waited for the boy to make up his mind while Steve set the port in circulation.

'Well, there was one thing. I don't suppose it's important, but when I left the Baxter cottage I thought I heard someone whistling.'

'Good,' Paul said promptingly.

'But I couldn't see anyone.'

'Never mind, John; you thought you heard someone. What did the whistling sound like?'

'I don't really know.' He laughed uncertainly. 'It was pretty tuneless, as if he was thinking about something else.'

'Not a wolf whistle, to attract attention?' Steve intervened.

'Good lord, no.'

'Pop or jazz?' Paul asked.

'Neither.'

'Ah,' said Paul quickly, 'so you did recognise the tune.'

The boy was confused. 'I didn't recognise it, Mr Temple.'

'But you're certain it wasn't a call or a pop song or a jazz theme. So you either recognised the tune itself or you thought you recognised the person who was whistling it.'

The boy shrugged unhappily. 'I'm not really sure,' he muttered, 'but I think it was Loch Lomond.'

'And whom did you think was whistling it?'

'I don't know.'

That was all Paul could elicit from Master John Draper. It almost seemed like a wasted evening. Paul didn't return to the subject until the Elk and his charge were leaving for the last train to Dulworth Bay.

'Tell me, John,' he said on the hotel steps, 'have you ever heard of anyone called Curzon?'

'No,' said the boy, 'I'm certain I haven't.'

'Never mind. It was kind of you to come. I've enjoyed meeting you. *Civic civicismus*, Mr Elkington.'

'Such a pleasure to discuss old times—'

The fishing fleet was coming into Whitby harbour. Paul and Steve walked along the jetty and watched the boats tying up amid the flurry of excited seagulls and the busy preparations for unloading the catch. It was a cool, dry evening and the light from either the moon or the harbour electricity was sharply clear.

'Impressive,' said Paul. 'I envy you a childhood spent among fishing fleets and countryside like this.' It was a comment which Paul made whenever he ventured north with his wife, because it always seemed to please her so inordinately. She had been extremely anxious that Yorkshire should meet with Paul Temple's approval.

'It seems,' she said wistfully, 'a very long time ago.'

Paul nodded. 'What did you make of young Draper?'

'Clever,' said Steve. 'Too clever by half. He knew exactly how to get round you. All that talk about the police . . .'

Paul was silent for a moment while they walked to the headland. 'Yes, I suppose you're right. He did seem to think that Elkington was a fool as well.'

Steve smiled to herself. 'Whereas you treated the Elk like a man of dignity and position.'

28

'Well, I always hated Latin at school.'

When they got back to the hotel Paul applied his mind to reviewing Dr Stern's book on crime. He sat at a table by the window making notes while Steve prepared for bed. He looked across at the quayside and watched the occasional movements of the boats, wondering whether to write a showy piece of invective or a considered essay on understanding the criminal's mind. He wondered who those sheep on the moors had belonged to and why the editor wanted the book reviewed anyway. He poured himself a large whisky and glanced through the index.

'Coincidence,' he said to Steve.

'Eh?' She was sitting up in bed, looking elegant in mauve silk pyjamas. 'What's a coincidence?'

'Dr Stern doesn't mention coincidence. You see, he knows nothing about crime. How many criminals would the law apprehend if it weren't for luck, chance and coincidence? Take the Great Train Robbery—'

'Are you doing that review?' asked Steve in dismay. 'But you haven't read the book yet!'

'I'd only make myself irritable and give the book a panning. I thought I might be generous and welcome this work as a tentative first step towards a more responsible attitude—'

'You pompous fraud,' said Steve.

They were interrupted by the strident ring of a telephone. Paul found the instrument on a chair beneath Steve's dressing-gown. It rang again. 'Hello?' said Paul. He looked at his watch and saw that it was nearly eleven o'clock.

'Mr Temple? Hello, this is Ian Elkington. I'm sorry if I woke you—'

'That's all right,' Paul said, 'I was only working.'

'Oh. I'm sorry, but the fact is that I've lost young Draper.'

'Lost him? Wasn't that rather difficult?'

'No— no, you don't understand. I mean the boy has vanished. We were in the train, walking through the corridor just north of Dulworth Bay, and suddenly I realised he'd gone. We were in the tunnel and the train was rattling rather. Draper was only a few yards ahead of me and at first I thought he'd nipped into the toilet. But he seems to have disappeared.'

Chapter Three

The Whitby to Scarborough train ran along the coast and probably qualified as the most beautiful stretch of track in England. The North Sea stretched away like an immobile sheet of blue on one side, while the inland view was of distant moors and forestry, sudden valleys with neatly arranged farms and a perilous hillside into which the railway lines were cut. They went through places like Burniston and Cloughton and Ravenscar, evocative places which suggested an England before the arrival of railways. There had been a furore of protest when the line had been built, and another a century later when someone had tried to close the line down.

The train chugged slowly through the scene, giving Paul and Steve ample time for leisured contemplation. Steve leaned forward occasionally to point out Farmer Hattersby's barn on the skyline and the village where old Mrs Stark had lived.

'We're just coming into the tunnel now, I think,' said Steve. 'This cliff ahead of us . . .'

The train curled round and into the face of the cliff, plunging the carriage in darkness. The noise of the engine and the wheels on the track seemed aggressively loud, but that wasn't the noise which Paul was listening to. He could hear somebody coming along the train corridor whistling tunelessly to himself. The whistling came nearer, stopped by their doors, and then came into the carriage.

'This is where John Draper disappeared,' said Steve.

'Quite,' murmured Paul.

The newcomer seemed to have sat in the corner of the carriage and was whistling an absent-minded version of Loch Lomond. Paul leaned across and placed a reassuring hand on Steve's knee. She gasped in alarm.

'It's all right, darling,' he said with a laugh, 'it's only your husband.' But he waited apprehensively, all his reflexes at the ready for whatever might happen in the fateful tunnel.

But nothing happened. Two minutes later the train chugged harmlessly into sunshine and Paul found himself staring at an elderly man with a quizzical smile and a deaf aid. The man looked a little startled himself to see Paul Temple.

'My goodness,' he said with that slightly overpitched tone of the very deaf, 'it's Mr Temple and his wife. Well— well.' He raised a hand to silence Paul while he adjusted his deaf aid. 'There, now you can speak. I'm afraid I'm a little hard of hearing.'

'How do you know—?' Paul began.

'I expect you're wondering how I know your name. By the way, I'm Dr Lawrence Stuart. I'm in practice in Dulworth Bay. We're all of us agog to see you in action. Local gossip has it that you'll solve the case in forty-eight hours.' He laughed. 'I think they're hoping you'll pin all three disappearances on me.'

'Lucky for you we're only here for a holiday,' said Paul. 'I promised Inspector Morgan he could pin the disappearances on the villain without interference from me.'

Dr Stuart chuckled happily. 'Yes, I heard about your little

pretext. I gather Mrs Temple was brought up in the North Riding? Wonderful place to spend your childhood, don't you think, Mr Temple?' He looked out of the window for the wide arc of Dulworth Bay to bear witness to his enthusiasm. The grey overhanging cliffs seemed by an optical illusion to be leaning into the distant sea. 'This rock face below us is worth a tourist's visit, Mr Temple,' he continued ironically. 'This is where we had the air disaster three weeks ago. You must have read about it. All the passengers were killed and we've been plagued by sightseers ever since.'

'I read about it,' said Paul.

'It happened just after midnight. I was called out of my bed. A most distressing business. They'd still be gossiping about it in the village if your Baxter boys hadn't disappeared to provide a new topic.'

'I wonder,' Paul said thoughtfully. 'You obviously know this community. Have you ever heard of anyone called Curzon?'

'No.' But the amused eyes, the face in constant movement, were impossible to read. 'I know everybody in Dulworth Bay, but I've never heard of Curzon, and I told Inspector Morgan the same when he asked me.'

'It must be very rewarding,' Steve said suddenly, 'to be the family doctor whom everybody knows and trusts in a village like Dulworth.'

Dr Stuart blinked in surprise. He almost stopped smiling. 'I may as well tell you now, Mrs Temple, before everyone else does, that I'm not very popular in Dulworth Bay. I'm a foreigner, from Edinburgh, and to make matters worse—'

'I'm sure they adore you,' Steve interrupted.

'No— no. They think I'm a good doctor, I'm pleased to say, but they're just a wee bit afraid of me.'

'Why should they be afraid of you, Dr Stuart?'

The doctor chuckled good-naturedly. 'Well, you see, a long time ago I murdered a man. And the people of Dulworth Bay are very conventional.'

The train was stopping at the station, a picturesque little wayside halt built in timber with the name Dulworth Bay picked out by stones in a flower bed and a man like Will Hay by the ticket office with a flag in his hand. Paul lifted Steve down on to the wooden platform and then waved goodbye to Dr Stuart.

'Can I give you a lift?' asked the doctor. 'My car is here in the forecourt.'

'No, thanks,' said Paul. 'We're only going to St Gilbert's School—'

'It's a half-hour walk. I'll give you a lift.' He ushered them across the tarmac to a battered Rover 2000, which seemed appropriate to his aura of collapsed opulence. 'I ought to visit St Gilbert's,' he said, 'they're suffering a wave of German measles. There's nothing I can do, but a visit from the doctor always goes down well. They like to think that you care.'

'Are you the school doctor?'

'Aye, of course.'

The car rattled its way up the perilously steep road from the village. The road was beside a stream which tumbled down to the bay and Paul watched anxiously as three small boys seemed to be dropping a fourth over a bridge. He turned to watch, but the scene was quickly lost in the clutter of untidy roofs, and then they were driving through the new sector of post war building which was carefully segregated at the top of the hill.

'I'm everybody's doctor in Dulworth Bay. Have been since I came here eleven years ago.'

'So you must know the Baxter brothers pretty well.'

He gave a teasing glance over his shoulder. 'Now you want to know whether they were worried recently, off their food or suffering from nervous illness, and the answer is no.'

'As I'm sure you told Inspector Morgan,' Paul completed with a laugh.

'Exactly. I also told him they were sober, earnest kids who wouldn't run off for a lark.'

St Gilbert's was an impressive eighteenth century building. The school had been founded by Edward VI in 1552 for sons of the deserving poor and had rapidly become extremely expensive. The building in front of them marked the transition from charity to privilege; it loomed up from the moorland with a sudden, sombre majesty.

'By the way,' said Dr Stuart, 'I hope you're not expecting to see the Reverend Dudley Clarke?'

'Why, is he away?'

'Aye, until Saturday morning. He's at some conference or other. I've never known a man spend so much of his time flitting from one place to another. You'd think he was a commercial traveller instead of the head of a public school.'

Paul smiled. 'You sound unimpressed by Dr Clarke.'

'He's a gas bag. He talks too much and says too little.'

'Never mind, we'll visit the Elk.'

Dr Stuart resumed his whistling of Loch Lomond. Just as the tuneless monotony was grating on Paul's nerves the doctor waved towards a dusty, overgrown road. 'That leads to the Baxter home,' he said. They were turning into the school grounds.

'We'll take a walk down there when we've seen the Elk.'

Dr Stuart drew up by the main entrance to let out Paul and Steve. 'Strange fellow,' Paul murmured as they stood on the top of the steps and watched him disappear in the direction of the sanatorium. 'He doesn't seem the murdering kind.'

The inside of the school was starkly institutional, with flagstone corridors, walls in green and cream, dimly lit and surgically clean. There seemed to be a great clattering of schoolboy shoes and a reverberation of treble voices.

'Can you show me Mr Elkington's study?' Paul asked a fresh-faced lad called, according to a spotty friend, Ursa Major.

They found Elkington in his room on the first floor of the east wing. It looked as though he had been marking the essays which were strewn across his table, but he was standing at his door grunting welcomes.

'I see you came with our eccentric doctor,' he said abstractedly. 'Good to see you again. Port?'

'I beg your pardon?'

'Port and biscuits, or do you prefer tea?'

'He'd prefer tea,' said Steve. 'Have you had any news of young Draper?'

'No,' said Elkington. He pottered about making tea from an electric kettle by the fireplace while Paul examined the oak bookcases and a framed photograph of the school first eleven, tapped the oak panelling and admired the elegant furniture. Elkington lived in the calm seclusion of an ivy-covered tower, and he was clearly out of his depth among murder and kidnapping. 'I've had the boy's parents on the telephone all day. They seem to think it was my fault.'

'They must think you a little careless,' said Paul unsympathetically. 'I can't understand why you didn't stop the train as soon as the boy disappeared.'

Elkington poured boiling water into the teapot while he considered his reasons. 'It took me some time before I realised what had happened,' he admitted at last. 'I searched the length of the train, but I didn't really know what to do. I thought that when we reached Dulworth he might leap out of the baggage compartment. But he didn't.'

Elkington could add nothing in the way of motive for young Draper's disappearance. The boy had simply vanished, and the inference had to be that he was kidnapped to prevent him telling what he knew to Paul Temple. Except that he was kidnapped after the visit instead of before . . . Paul tried to remember precisely what the boy had said.

'The main item was that somebody had been in the lane when the boys went back to the school.'

'And that somebody,' Steve said brightly, 'was probably Dr Stuart.'

'It's a possibility,' Paul said cautiously. 'Although we mustn't jump to conclusions.' He wondered briefly whether Dulworth Bay could have more than one man who whistled tunelessly while he was going about his business. 'What sort of doctor do you find him?' Paul asked the Elk.

Elkington sat in one of the massive armchairs and pursed his lips. There was, it seemed, a story connected with Dr Stuart. Elkington stirred his tea and began to tell it.

'Apparently about fifteen years ago Dr Stuart was quite a big noise in Harley Street. Then suddenly, for some unaccountable reason, he started drinking heavily. Which didn't matter until one night when he was called out to do an emergency operation.'

'Don't tell me,' said Paul, 'let me guess. The doctor was drunk and the patient died?'

Elkington looked surprised. 'That's right. How did you—?'

'I wrote that story twenty years ago,' Paul said with a laugh. 'And even then I didn't sell it. Of all the corny old chestnuts!'

'Well, that's what happened,' said Elkington. 'Everybody in the village will tell you so.'

The sun was still shining when they left the school, which surprised Paul. He had forgotten in the gloomy precincts of the Elk's study that it was a summer afternoon. He slipped his arm through Steve's and listened to her talk of childhood as they walked along the winding lane to the Baxter house. They paused to pat a horse on the nose. The smell of grass and the dust from the lane hung lazily in the air.

'Let's go riding tomorrow,' said Steve. 'I know a farmer with several horses we could—'

'We're here to find those missing boys,' Paul began.

'We're here on holiday, remember? Oh look, there's a haystack. Have you ever made love in a haystack?'

'No,' Paul said promptly. He knew the diplomatic answer; Steve was inclined to be resentful of her husband's life when she had been wearing pigtails.

'There was a terribly realistic love scene in that novel you wrote two years ago, full of the damp heat of the hay and bodies perspiring with passion—'

'Pure imagination,' Paul said hastily.

'I thought you went out with a farmer's daughter when you were eighteen.'

'Yes,' Paul agreed. 'I once kissed her sitting on a bale of hay. We thought that was pretty daring.'

Steve had been looking speculatively at the yellow haystack, but the sudden appearance of a farm labourer with a pitch fork in his hand dispelled any notions of romance. 'Come on,' she said decisively, 'this is no place for dalliance.'

They reached a bend in the lane and came upon what Paul decided was a hamlet. About a dozen small cottages, a general stores, a pub and a tiny church. 'World's End,' Steve murmured inexplicably. She paused to watch a dog climb lazily to its feet, stretch itself and amble towards them. She spun round in a dizzy imitation of joy. 'I used to know a boy who lived in one of those cottages. My first big devastating romance. I forget which cottage. But I was going to marry him. Billy, I think his name was, or Charley, something like that. He was terribly tough and masculine, with blond hair and freckles—'

'When was this?' Paul demanded.

'Oh, before I met you, darling.' She took his arm and walked sprightly across the grass to the general stores. There was a notice board in the window with several card advertisements. 'No need to be jealous. He was seven and I was six. He had a fight with the boy my mother paired me off with, and he won me. The other boy ran away when his nose started bleeding.' She laughed and looked up into Paul's face. 'You've never fought for my hand, have you?'

Paul glared. 'I often have to restrain myself from punching your friends on the nose.' He looked intently at the advertisements. Women could be very tiresome. '£5 Reward. Lost. Parrot, with red and green plumage, answers to the name of Cheeta. Apply within.' Oh well, the shop was closed anyway. 'What did you say your grand passion's name was?'

'Charley, I think, although it might have been Jimmy.'

They walked through the hamlet and on down the lane. There were several large, pretentiously Victorian houses with many acres of overgrown garden on the road beyond. One of these was presumably the Baxter cottage. It was the kind of property a stockbroker might retire to, although the word cottage was a trifle euphemistic.

Paul led the way through a tangle of rose bushes and wild irises to the front door. He rang the bell and heard it echo hollowly inside the house. While he waited he peered inquisitively through the lattice bay windows, then he rang again. The house appeared to be empty.

'Look,' said Steve, 'the door's open.'

Paul glanced back over his shoulder to see who was coming. 'They do things like that in the country. They believe in being neighbourly.' There was nobody coming so he went boldly into the house.

It was one of those labyrinthine buildings where you lose all sense of the outer four walls. There were sudden rooms at the turn of a staircase, passages vanishing into unexpected corners. They twice found themselves in the study and they couldn't find the kitchen. In the morning-room there was a half-drunk cup of warm tea, as though somebody had been in the house until recently.

'Anybody home?' Paul called.

'Creek eek!' came the answer from somewhere behind them.

'Who's that?'

'Cheek!'

Paul hurried into the hall and received a momentary shock from the sight of himself and Steve hurrying towards him. It was a tall, very dark mercury looking-glass. The inhuman call, 'Cheeka – a – cheek!' guided them to the room beyond the wide flight of stairs.

'Hello,' squeaked the voice as they entered the living-room. 'Hello, hello, hello.' It preened its yellow and green feathers as it spoke.

'It's a parrot,' Paul said with relief. 'Good afternoon.' The parrot stared back silently. 'Is that your unfinished cup of tea in the other room?'

No answer.

'Perhaps it doesn't like men,' said Steve. She pushed a finger through its cage and tickled its neck. 'Hello,' she said in that voice which she normally reserved for small children. 'What's your name?'

'Cheet – a – cheet!' it squawked.

'That's a funny name.'

'Cheeta,' it repeated angrily.

Paul laughed. 'People do give parrots ridiculous names. There was that card in the window down the lane – answers to the name of Cheeta.' His laughter stopped abruptly. 'What did it say its name was?'

'Cheeta!' squawked the parrot.

'Do you realise—?'

Yes,' Steve agreed patiently, 'that was the name of the missing parrot.' She continued tickling the feathers on its neck. 'But if it's supposed to be lost, what on earth is it doing here?'

'Your guess,' Paul said thoughtfully, 'is as good as mine.'

They were interrupted by a dull thud from upstairs. It sounded as though somebody was moaning, and another thud sent Paul running towards the stairs. 'Quickly,' he called to Steve, 'there's something wrong.'

'Probably another parrot trying to escape.'

Paul halted abruptly at the foot of the stairs. There was a man above him, hauling himself to his feet by the rails on the landing. His face was dripping with blood, and he was groaning with the pain and effort. The man was clearly out on his feet.

'Stay where you are!' Paul shouted.

The man gaped down unseeingly, swayed slightly back and then lurched forward on to the bannisters. They broke beneath his weight. Without a murmur the man plunged fifteen feet to land beside Paul on the bottom stair.

'Is he dead?' Steve asked.

The man was limply heavy as Paul lifted his head and then let him roll on to his back. 'He's been very savagely beaten.' Even tortured, Paul thought. He examined the man's neck and ribs. Somebody had a pretty thorough knowledge of how to cause serious damage. Paul stood up in disgust and then went upstairs to the main bedroom.

'Is he Mr Baxter?' asked Steve.

'Yes.' Paul pointed to a photograph on the dressing-table.

It was a family group: two boys, an attractive middle-aged mother and the dead man looking plumply prosperous. 'He was Baxter.'

The telephone began ringing beside the bed downstairs in the hall. Paul sighed. 'Shall we answer it?' He sat on the bed and picked up the receiver. 'Hello?' He glanced at the number on the dial. 'This is Dulworth 9862.'

'Is that you, father?' asked a youthful voice.

'Mm,' Paul mumbled as non-commitlally as possible. 'Who's that speaking?'

'Michael of course! Old Tom said he saw the card in the shop window about the parrot. Father, can we come home now?'

Paul paused while he wondered what this meant. 'When did old Tom see the card?'

'This afternoon on his way back from work.' The boy sounded suddenly suspicious. 'Your voice sounds different,' he said. 'Is anything the matter, father?'

'No— no, nothing,' Paul said quickly. 'Where are you speaking from?'

'Why, from the box near Tom's place.' There was a brief silence. 'Who are you? Is my father all right?' His voice was rising in alarm. 'I want to know what's going on!'

'Put me on to Tom,' said Paul. 'Is he there?'

'Hang on.' There was a whispered consultation at the other end of the line, and then another, older voice with a Yorkshire accent spoke a sullen, 'Yes, who's that?'

'Now listen,' Paul said with all the authority he could project, 'don't ring off, whatever you do! My name's Temple. I don't know what this is all about, but you must believe what I'm telling you. Baxter is dead. He's been murdered.'

For a moment Paul could hear nothing but the man's breathing. 'I don't believe it,' he said eventually. 'It's a trap to get the boys.'

'I'm afraid not,' said Paul. 'You'd better bring them here and explain yourself to the police. Now will you kindly clear the line? I have several telephone calls to make.' He replaced the receiver and looked up at Steve in some perplexity. 'Do you understand what that was all about?' he asked her.

'No.'

'Neither do I. Unless Baxter was involved in the kidnapping of his own children.'

Chapter Four

Inspector Morgan was still rigidly polite, but it was a notice-
able effort for him. He snapped at the two police constables
on duty by the cottage door, swore at the police photographer
and grumbled bitterly because the finger print expert was
late on the scene. But he said please and thank you to Paul,
and made ironic small talk with Steve.

'I suppose,' he said while Dr Stuart was examining the body,
'that you won't be coming up here for your holidays very often?'

'Good Lord no,' said Paul, 'I prefer a quiet life!'

'I hadn't noticed,' Steve murmured wryly.

The inspector wandered restlessly across to the front door.

The two uniformed constables fidgeted nervously until he
returned to watch the medical examination. 'What makes you
so sure this man Tom will bring the boys back?' he asked
bleakly. 'If I were Tom I'd get the hell out of Yorkshire before
we find out who he is.'

'You'll see,' said Paul. 'He'll be here soon.'

The inspector muttered something about psychological
intuition as he went off to curse the photographer. The
photographer was leaning precariously over the fractured
bannisters to achieve an aerial view of the corpse.

'The boys will have some packing to do,' Paul said with a glance at his watch, 'before they come and face this ordeal.' But he was feeling apprehensive. He might be completely mistaken.

Dr Stuart looked up from the body, tuned in his deaf aid, and pronounced that Baxter was dead. 'Broken neck,' he said, 'in layman's terms. Poor old fellow. Been dead for about half an hour, I suppose.' He replaced his instruments in the bag and prepared to go. 'I'll let you have the certificate tomorrow morning, Inspector.'

'Aye, that'll be soon enough.'

The doctor paused and looked sadly at Paul. 'Why should anyone want to murder Philip Baxter, eh? Isn't it always the decent friendly people who come to an unfortunate end? I've known Philip Baxter for years. A nicer man you couldn't wish to have met.'

Paul followed him to the front door. 'When did you first meet Baxter then?'

'A long time ago. He was a stockbroker in London when I first knew him. But he had one or two lucky breaks and then retired early in life. I suppose he would be only fifty or fifty-one now. Quite young.' He led the way down the front path and then stopped to watch a large estate car bumping along the lane. 'Oh dear,' he said, 'I'd been hoping to miss the arrival of the boys. I don't like grief.'

'You're in the wrong job,' Paul said tensely. It was a scene he too would have preferred to miss.

The estate car slithered to a halt and two teenage boys climbed out of the passenger seats looking rigidly impassive. Paul stood aside as they went silently into the cottage. At the wheel of the car was a middle aged man with a florid, weather beaten face.

'Good Lord,' said Dr Stuart, 'it's old Tom Doyle.'

The uniformed constables had moved unobtrusively from the cottage to positions on either side of the car. 'I think you'd better come inside, Mr Doyle,' said one of them. 'The inspector will want to ask you some questions.'

Doyle nodded. 'But we'll give the boys a few minutes alone with him, shall we? They don't need an audience.' He took his pipe from his jacket pocket and filled it with slow deliberation. Then he sat puffing thoughtfully and staring into infinity while the few minutes ticked by.

A squirrel ran along the branch of a tree opposite and jumped fully seven feet before vanishing into the swaying foliage of a chestnut tree. Paul followed its path by the movement of the leaves and a few moments later he saw it flying through the air again. It sent him into a reverie about Beatrix Potter, until suddenly Dr Stuart spoke.

'Ah well,' the doctor said, 'I'll go and look to the two laddies. They'll maybe need a sedative.' He went reluctantly along the path. 'They might do best to board at St Gilbert's for a while. I can speak to the senior master.'

Steve passed him in the doorway as she emerged looking slightly distraught. She hurried to Paul and took his arm, but then she waited several seconds before she spoke. 'Darling,' she said at last, 'I've offered to stay here for a while. The boys have an aunt living in Leeds and we've sent her a telegram. But in the meantime I'll cook their supper and generally stay around. They have a few friends who could help out, but they're both being incredibly stoical and they won't impose on people they know.' Once she had started she spoke in a rush with the sentences crowding in upon each other until Paul said reassuringly, 'Whoa! Yes, yes, I think that's a splendid idea. Good for you, darling.'

He kissed her cheek. 'Inspector Morgan can give me a lift into Whitby.'

An ambulance arrived to take away the body. Police formalities had apparently been completed and the inspector led his colleagues from the cottage with the stretcher party.

'I suppose you'll be staying here with your wife, Mr Temple?' he asked without conviction.

'Actually no, I was going to ask you—'

'All right, get in the car!' He turned angrily to the uniformed men by the estate car. 'Come on, you two, let's have Doyle down at the station then!'

Tom Doyle was an enigmatic man. He was popular and also a little mysterious, kind-hearted and private. He was a fisherman and odd-job man and adventurer. But the village accepted him, which probably proved that he was sound. He seemed honest enough to Paul as he sat puffing his pipe in the inspector's office.

'So tell us about the Baxter boys,' said the inspector. 'Why have they been hiding?'

'I don't know.' There was an air of baffled sincerity in his voice. 'I swear I don't know, and that's the truth!'

One evening about three weeks ago Tom Doyle had returned from a day's fishing, and there had been a message asking him to call round and see Mr Baxter. 'He'd just bought a lot of plants from one of the local nurseries and I knew he wanted me to sort them out for him. Market gardening's by way of being a hobby of mine.' So Doyle had gone along to the cottage at around eight o'clock.

When he reached the cottage he found Mr Baxter standing in the doorway talking to Lord Westerby and another well-built man with an American accent. Baxter was looking worried, harassed even, and he didn't notice the odd-job man at his gate. 'All right, all right,' he was saying wearily, 'if that's the way it is.'

'Indeed it is, Baxter. I think we've made the position clear.'

'And I hope there's no bad feeling,' said the American. You understand there's nothing personal about all this.'

Baxter nodded. 'The position is quite clear and there's nothing personal. I know.'

The American was clearly dissatisfied with Baxter's weary resignation, but Lord Westerby thought they had made their point. 'Come along, Walters, we must be going. He sees our view of the matter, even if he doesn't appreciate it.'

'That isn't enough. I'll give him until Friday of next week, and then I'll—'

'Now now, Walters, there's no need to threaten him.'

'Well, there's an awful lot of money tied up in this deal. We gotta be careful!'

Lord Westerby was coming along the path towards Doyle. 'Evening, Tom,' Lord Westerby said with hearty benevolence. 'How's the world treating you?' He seemed not at all put out that their conversation might have been overheard.

'Mustn't grumble, sir,' said Doyle.

'Really? Why not? I grumble all the time!' His lordship bellowed with laughter, wrapped his tweed jacket across his ample tummy, and strode off to the Land Rover parked beside the chestnut tree. The American followed looking less pleased with life.

'If there's no news on Friday,' he said severely to Lord Westerby, 'you'll just have to come down to London.'

'Don't be impatient, my dear fellow.' He started up the engine and then waved to Baxter and Doyle. 'Cheerio!' He smiled indulgently at the man called Walters. 'I mean to say, whatever happens we must try not to be stupid about this business.' The Land Rover sent up a cloud of dust and then roared off along the country lane.

Philip Baxter watched them go with pensive apprehension. He looked, old Tom Doyle thought to himself, as if the noble Westerby was asking for the leasehold back on his home. He didn't even say hello to Tom Doyle. 'Come in and have a drink,' he said inaudibly.

'Thanks,' said Doyle as he followed into the cottage. 'I suppose you want to see me about those plants—'

'Some other time.' Philip Baxter went through to the kitchen. 'I'd been saving this brandy for a special occasion,' he said sadly, 'but we'll drink it, shall we? It's better than all those gut-rotting whiskies they sell in the grocers' shops. And I don't have any beer.'

Tom Doyle was mystified, but he raised his glass and asked what they were celebrating. He spoke with cheerful reassurance. And when Baxter looked forlorn he offered to help. 'If there's anything I can do,' he said stoutly.

Baxter sat in the winged armchair and sipped a large brandy. For several minutes he didn't speak. Then he sighed. 'Do you like my boys, Tom? Do you think Roger and Michael are worth sacrificing my life for?'

'They're a fine couple of boys, Mr Baxter,' he said in bewilderment.

Baxter stared into his glass again, noticed it was empty and refilled it. Then he stared at the glowing golden liquid.

'They aren't in any kind of trouble, are they?' Doyle asked. 'Roger and Michael? Are they all right?'

Baxter shook his head. 'I wonder,' he said thoughtfully. 'Do you think they could stay with you for a while, Tom? Perhaps for two or three weeks?'

To begin with Doyle had thought he meant a holiday. Trips on the boat and roughing it in the morning getting breakfast for themselves. But Baxter had been in earnest. They were to stay with old Tom Doyle and stay out of sight.

'It's not a holiday, Tom. I'm not going away. But I want the boys to disappear.' He finished the brandy in one tasteless gulp. 'I don't want them to go to school, I don't want them to be seen about the village, and I don't want anyone to know they're staying with you.'

'You want me to hide them?' he asked nervously. 'But why?' Doyle laughed. 'The lads can't just disappear like that. There'll be all sorts of questions asked. What will the school say? Why, the police might even get to hear of it, and then there'll be a lot of awkward questions asked!'

'The police will certainly get to hear of it, Tom, because I intend to report the matter to them.'

Doyle was no longer amused. 'What do you mean?'

'I want to give the impression that the boys have either run away from home or been abducted. I'll kick up all the fuss I know how, with the local press and anybody else I can think of.'

Doyle nodded fatalistically. 'And all the time they'll be in my cottage? I don't like it.'

'They're in danger, Tom, and there's nothing else I can do about it. I'd go to the police if I could, but—' He was drumming his fingers nervously on the arm of the chair. 'I'm sorry I can't explain, but this is the only solution.'

Doyle went thoughtfully across to the window and looked at the box of new potted plants in the conservatory. 'Supposing I do what you want,' he said slowly. 'Supposing I take the boys in and hide them for three or four weeks, how do we know that by then things will have changed? Can we be sure that this danger will have blown over?'

Baxter could see that he had persuaded his man. 'We can't, Tom, but in three or four weeks I shall be able to cope with the situation.'

'And what will you tell the boys?'

'The truth.'

Baxter had gone to the drawer of his desk in the next room and taken a hundred pounds in ten pound notes from a cash tin. 'That'll pay for all expenses,' he said, 'and whatever is left over is yours.' He had waved aside Doyle's protests. 'Now remember, once the boys arrive at your cottage I don't want them to get in touch with me, and neither must you. On no account must you call, write or telephone. Is that clearly understood?'

Doyle sighed and put the money in his pocket. 'Yes, Mr Baxter. But supposing something happens, some emergency? One of them might be taken ill—'

'You know the little shop in the lane? Mrs Vernon's? If you need me put a card in the window: "Three-wheeler bike for sale, two spare tyres, suitable for boy of ten".'

'And if you want me?' asked Doyle.

'I shan't want you, Tom. But keep an eye on the shop. When you see a card reading: "£5 Reward. Lost Parrot, red and green plumage, answers to the name of Cheeta", then you'll know the coast is clear. Throw your hat in the air and ask Michael to telephone me.'

That was all Tom Doyle could tell them. 'The boys turned up at five o'clock the following afternoon and they stayed with me until today – until I saw the card in the window.'

Inspector Morgan glowered at the man, reluctant to send him home but clearly having no grounds for an arrest. 'What about this other boy, this John Draper?' he asked without much optimism. 'Where has he vanished to?'

'I've no idea.' Doyle leaned forward anxiously. 'I read about his disappearance in the newspaper and it frightened the life out of me. But Mr Baxter couldn't have been involved in that, sir.'

'Why not?'

Doyle turned nervously to Paul and shrugged his shoulders. 'Well, he couldn't, could he? I mean, he didn't say anything to me about young Draper. Just his own boys.'

'I'm sure you're right,' Paul murmured reassuringly. 'Did Mr Baxter say anything to you about Curzon?'

'No, sir.'

Paul smiled and rose to his feet. It had been an illuminating interview, but it was time to go. Paul found the atmosphere of provincial police stations oppressive; they had all been built in 1870, which was not his favourite period in architecture.

Paul Temple went back to the hotel and collected his car. He needed to think. He drove across the moors weighing up in his mind all the facts he knew about the Curzon case and noting all the questions for which he had no answer.

He knew that Doyle had been a convincing witness, and his story had been circumstantial. Philip Baxter had obviously hidden the boys with him because of some threat, and the threat had been real enough because Baxter himself was dead. Was it something to do with the business arrangement between Baxter and Lord Westerby?

Somebody had three times tried to kill Diana Maxwell and she was afraid for her life. She wouldn't talk after all, but perhaps her uncle, Lord Westerby, would know what was troubling her.

And who was Curzon? His name had been on Roger's cricket bat, and Diana Maxwell had originally claimed to know all about him. Paul watched the sun disappear below the greens and browns of the distant horizon leaving behind it a chilly golden glow. There was no good reason for thinking that Curzon was important, except for Charlie Vosper's nose.

The Baxter cottage looked the same as it had before the tragedy. Paul found it difficult to believe that violence had erupted behind those curtained windows. He knocked on the door and half expected Philip Baxter to open it and explain that it had all been a mistake.

But in fact it was Steve who came to let him in.

She raised a finger to her lips. 'The boys are just having supper,' she said confidentially. 'You won't start interrogating them now, will you? They're still rather numb from shock.'

Paul went into the cottage. 'It's my wife I've come to see. I haven't eaten this evening, and apart from you this whole county is packed out with Yorkshire people. I was feeling lonely.' He found his way to the kitchen, where two youthful faces looked up at him, paused, and then continued eating. 'If there's a scrap of cold meat left over,' Paul said, 'or a small piece of cheese—'

'Roger and Michael have healthy appetites. But there's half a Yorkshire pudding,' Steve said cruelly, 'and a can of beer in the fridge.'

The two boys smiled shyly and watched Steve prepare a pile of ham sandwiches. 'We've been talking about you this evening,' said the younger of them. 'I edit the school magazine and Mrs Temple was telling me about your early days as a writer. I'd like to be a novelist.'

Paul laughed. 'You'd do better to find a proper job. Why not be a professional cricketer? Then you can be a sports journalist when you retire.'

'To be a good cricketer,' the boy said tactlessly, 'is damned hard work.'

It appeared that Steve had established real sympathy with the Baxter boys. The older one, Michael, had questioned her on the life and prospects of a designer and they had discussed his intention of going to art school in London next year. He was an engaging young man who had known something of Steve's reputation from a newspaper article just after Christmas.

'He was about to take me upstairs to show me his port-folio,' said Steve.

Paul raised an ironic eyebrow. 'All right. Roger and I can stay down here and talk about cricket. I hate eating sand-wiches by myself.' He turned man to man and asked Roger whether he played for the school first eleven.

'No,' said Roger when they were alone. 'I'm not really good enough. That's why I thought I'd be a novelist.'

Paul munched thoughtfully on a ham sandwich for several seconds. 'I was meaning to ask you, Roger, about a name on your cricket bat. Why did you add the name Curzon to the school team?'

Roger Baxter gaped in astonishment. 'That was clever of you, Mr Temple! Fancy your noticing that!'

Paul shrugged modestly. 'What I call nose-ology.'

'I was only doodling,' the boy explained. 'I was supposed to be asleep, but it was a warm night and I wrote the name on the bat to pass the time. A lot of boys did that this term.'

'But why Curzon?' Paul insisted. 'I think it might be very important in helping to find out who killed your father. So please tell me what happened that night when you were supposed to be asleep.'

Roger Baxter blinked earnestly. 'Well, there's nothing much to tell. It was late, as I said, and I could hear voices downstairs. The voices were loud and angry, so I crept out on to the landing to find out what was happening.

'My father was downstairs in the living-room and there was another man with him. I didn't recognise the voice, but they were very angry with each other and my father kept on shouting, "I don't care what Curzon says! I'm not obeying these instructions whatever Curzon wants!" The quarrel went on for several minutes.' Roger smiled apologetically. 'My father never quarrelled with people. He hardly ever shouted, even at me.'

'And what did the other man say?'

'He said something about it being useless to argue. "Curzon calls the tune and we have to dance to it." That sort of thing. "Don't be stupid, Baxter, we all have to do as we're told." I found it very worrying. That was why I went back to my room and wrote the name on the cricket bat. I was thinking.'

'Did you ask your father what had been going on?'

'Yes, next morning at breakfast I asked who Curzon was. But father didn't tell me. At first he was extremely angry that I'd heard. Then he calmed down and said I should forget all about it. He said an old friend had dropped in for a drink and they were having a friendly argument.' The boy thought for a moment. 'But I don't know who the friend was. And he wasn't very friendly.'

The beer gave off a minor explosion as Paul opened the can and then poured it into a glass. 'What sort of voice did the man have?'

'Well spoken, educated. I suppose it was a southern accent.'

'Did your father ever mention a friend of his called Walters?' Paul asked. 'Damn and blast!' He had allowed the beer to fizz up and overflow on to the table. 'That's one reason I prefer whisky.'

'Walters?' the boy repeated. 'No, I've never heard father speak of him.' He leaned forward with sudden intensity. Tell me, Mr Temple, do you think this man Curzon murdered my father?'

Paul sighed. 'I wish I could be sure, Roger. But we'll soon know.' He dabbed the pool of beer with his napkin and then left the table. 'Ah well, that was delicious.' He took the remains of the drink into the next room.

It had been Philip Baxter's study and the aura of scholarship hung mustily in the air. A massive leather topped desk looked on to the gardens and beyond across the Westerby estates. It was the sort of room that Paul could never work in, with thick sound proof carpets and curtains like tapestry, wallpaper embossed with velvet. There were argumentative pre-Raphaelite paintings in heavy frames and packed, untidy bookcases. Paul wondered what Baxter had worked at during his retirement. The two volumes of the current *Stock Exchange Yearbook* looked unused and dust lay on the dictionary. The complete works of Trollope glistened artificially as if they had never been read.

'Did your father normally keep the odd hundred pounds in notes in the house?' Paul asked.

'No, he didn't. I was surprised when Tom said that father had taken the cash from his desk. But if Tom said so—'

Paul tried the drawers and found them open. But there was no cash box. The usual assortment of files and personal papers which Paul hadn't the nerve to read at that moment. He did glance at Baxter's cheque book, however, and found no counterfoil for withdrawals to account for a hundred pounds.

'My father thought that cash lying about was being wasted. He would have invested it or spent it.'

Paul nodded. He swivelled round in the padded chair behind the desk and snatched at *Barchester Towers* as he passed. The spines of ten novels by Trollope swung away from the bookshelves in one piece like a door. Behind the fake books was a wall safe.

'Well well well,' said Paul. 'Did you know this was here?'

'Yes, of course. When I first found it I tried to crack the combination. I'd been reading Edgar Wallace and I thought it ought to be easy, listening for the right digits to fall into place and all that. But I never managed it. I've no idea what father kept in there.'

'When was it installed?'

'I suppose about a year ago. That was when the complete works of Trollope appeared, and some of the books are real. Father read *The Prime Minister* over Christmas. I thought he intended going in for politics.'

Paul fiddled for several minutes with the combination while he wondered where the smell of burning was coming from. But if the safe had defeated a determined fourteen-year-old, he decided, it was unlikely that he would open it in a spare five minutes. The job needed special tools: a stethoscope or a charge of gelignite.

'I think something's on fire,' Roger announced suddenly.

'That's all right,' Paul said flippantly, 'you'll get used to my wife's cooking.'

'We thought she was a very good cook.'

'Yes, actually she is.' Paul looked about him in surprise. 'By God, I think the house is on fire!' There was a crackle of burning which became a roar as he ran into the hallway. Flames were leaping and snapping down the stairs and he saw that the upper part of the house was blazing uncontrollably.

'Paul!' he heard Steve shout from behind the fire. 'Are you all right?'

'Yes!' he called. 'Can you get down?'

'No, the stairs are going!'

As she spoke the bannisters folded in a shower of fireworks and the top flight crashed down into the hall. Smoke was billowing down the stair well and making it impossible to breathe. Paul found that his eyes were smarting and his whole body was wet with perspiration.

'The roof,' Roger Baxter called. 'You can climb out of the back window on to the roof!'

'Did you hear that?' Paul shouted.

'Yes.'

Paul hurriedly followed the younger brother into the garden. The whole lawn was floodlit by the flames. Paul peered up into the raging furnace and could just make out two silhouetted figures on the low protruding roof above the kitchen.

'Jump!' shouted Paul. 'This is no time for caution!' The effort of shouting filled his lungs with burning smoke and he choked briefly until a section of chimney tumbled on to the grass beside him.

Michael Baxter shinned rapidly down the drainpipe, using the kitchen window ledge with the expertise of a child who has practised the route before. Steve jumped at Paul's outstretched arms and they tumbled into a heap in the rhododendron bushes.

'Sorry, darling,' she murmured. 'Your new suit as well.'

'Damn my new suit. Are you all right?'

'Yes,' she said. 'How about the boys?'

The Baxter brothers were standing together a safe distance from the house. They were watching in silence. Too many things had happened to them for one day, and there was nothing much to be said. They simply watched while their home was consumed like a beacon in the night.

'We didn't get a chance to telephone the fire brigade,' said Paul.

Steve shrugged. 'It would take more than a few fire engines to put this lot out,' she said. 'It's such an old house, and there hasn't been much rain this summer.'

People were beginning to arrive in the lane, a large car drew up and voices could be heard asking each other whether anybody was inside. The two brothers took no notice, so Paul edged his way round the house to reassure the spectators and persuade somebody to send for the police.

'Yes yes,' he agreed, 'it's a fire. No, we all got out in time. It is most unfortunate.' In the face of a natural disaster such as this the questions were all well-meaning and the expressions of shock a trifle stereotyped. It wasn't an occasion for originality. 'Indeed we might have been burnt to death,' he agreed, 'but we're all alive. I wonder whether you could pop back home and telephone the police?'

The large car was parked on the far side of the road. 'Hello, Mr Temple!' a girl's voice called from the passenger seat. 'What's happening?'

Paul went across to Diana Maxwell. 'I'm afraid there's been a fire,' he said wearily. The driver of the car was Peter Malo. 'Fancy you two being in the vicinity,' he said. 'Taking a drive?'

'We saw the fire from the hall,' said Peter Malo, 'so we came to see whether we could help.'

'I suppose you didn't think of sending for the fire brigade?'

The young man laughed. 'Good Lord, yes. We gave them a ring as soon as we saw the flames, didn't we, Di?'

Diana Maxwell was watching Paul thoughtfully. 'Yes,' she said automatically, 'they should be here any minute now.'

Diana Maxwell climbed from the car. 'Will you wait here, Peter? I must have a quick word with Michael Baxter.' She took Paul Temple's arm and walked with him back to the house. She clung to him as they passed the raging debris of the conservatory. 'I wanted to talk with you privately, Mr Temple,' she said. 'I don't want Peter Malo to hear.'

'About Curzon?' he asked.

'Yes, if you like. Can you spare an hour sometime tomorrow?'

'We seem to have made appointments like this before.'

Her body stiffened at the criticism, but her tone was suitably amenable as she answered. 'I know, I'm sorry. I usually spend my summer days on our yacht out in the bay. It's more private than Westerby Hall. Can you come out tomorrow morning?'

'I'll try,' said Paul. 'What do you call this yacht?'

'*Windswept*,' she said with a toss of her hair. 'Ask any of the local fishermen, they'll take you out to it.'

Diana Maxwell left him on the lawn and went over to talk with Michael Baxter. At that moment the fire brigade arrived with an urgent clanging of bells. There were two tenders, and almost at once the crowds were being moved back and the house was surrounded by busy men in uniforms with a job to do.

'Stand back, please!' they were calling. 'Bring it through here, Turner! That's it, Wilson, straight through to join number eight!' Great jets of water soared up into the remnants of the roof while other firemen hacked away at the charred wood and plasterwork with their axes.

But they were too late to save much from the ruins. Somebody seemed to have ventured inside the house, and occasional chairs and pieces of blazing furniture were being tossed through the windows. Paul hoped rather cynically that Philip Baxter had been fully insured.

'We shall have to do something about those trees, sir,' a fireman called out.

The trees were ranged along the edge of the garden, and Paul just had time to pull Steve clear as a jet of water was redirected over their heads and into the foliage. 'They should have been sprayed already,' somebody said angrily. 'Stand clear, you two!' But the warning was too late.

'Never mind,' said Steve. 'It's cool, isn't it?'

They ran across to the dry safety beside Diana Maxwell and the two boys, then wiped the spray from their clothes and faces with handkerchiefs. Meanwhile the men inside the house were leaving for the last time. The walls were about to collapse.

'I'm taking Michael and Roger back to Westerby Hall,' said Diana Maxwell. 'Your wife has been very kind, but after this they need somewhere to stay while they put their lives back together.'

The two boys said goodbye and thank you, then followed the girl meekly away to the car. Paul watched them go feeling apprehensive and helpless. They might well be walking into the centre of danger.

'You mean they've been safe until now?' Steve asked ironically. 'There's only one way to make Dulworth Bay safe for them, and that's to clear up this case as quickly as possible. Shall we go?'

'In a moment,' said Paul. 'I want to pluck something from the ruins, if it survives the fire.'

He went across to the west wall of the house, a jagged pile of masonry that had fallen inwards and was still smoking, flaring up suddenly and moving with its own internal fire. He tried to guess where the study had been.

'What are you looking for?' asked Steve.

'This,' said Paul. He kicked aside a pile of smouldering rubble to something that lay gleaming among the burnt wood. It was a steel box, and as he turned it over with his foot Paul saw the combination lock that he had tried to open in the study. 'This is Philip Baxter's safe.'

'Whatever was in there,' said Steve, 'it'll be charred to a cinder now.'

'Maybe.' Paul carried it carefully on to the grass and then dropped it. 'Ouch!' He rubbed his hands painfully. 'That was hot.'

The safe was still intact and impossible to open. Paul glanced about him to see who was watching, but the firemen were still busy with the last of the crumbling walls. Paul picked up a brick and battered at the steel three inches to the left of the lock. As he raised the brick above his head for a further assault somebody gripped his wrist.

'Good evening, Mr Temple. Lost the key to your safe?'

It was Inspector Morgan, looking profoundly displeased.

'I was saying to my sergeant as we drove here tonight, well at least that chap Temple is in Whitby because we took him there ourselves. But I didn't really believe it. As soon as I heard there was trouble I guessed you would be here. Good evening, Mrs Temple. Very warm this evening.'

When they got back to the police station in Whitby it was extremely late, but Inspector Morgan didn't seem perturbed. He picked up the telephone, demanded two cups of cocoa from someone, and then sprawled back in his chair. 'Sit down, Temple, relax. I had a conversation with Charlie

Vosper this evening and he told me something you might find of interest.'

They were interrupted by a thump on the door and a dauntingly square shaped woman police constable brought in the cocoa. 'This'll make you sleep, love, if it doesn't kill you,' she said to Paul.

'It's too late for humour,' snapped Inspector Morgan. 'Send young Masterson in with his safe-cracking equipment.'

The woman stared at the safe on the desk. 'He isn't on duty, sir. Shall I have a go at it?'

Inspector Morgan said yes so she went off to fetch whatever precision instruments were required.

'We keep abreast of all the criminal skills, Temple,' he said proudly. 'That's how a copper keeps in the race, we can think like criminals and we can do their job better than they can themselves. Now, what were we saying?'

'Charlie Vosper. You were saying he told you—'

'Ah yes. Inspector Vosper is taking a long distance interest in this trouble. We were having a chat this evening, and I told him about Tom Doyle's story. I mentioned this American who was seen with Lord Westerby the evening before the boys disappeared. And do you know what?'

Paul tried to look guileless. 'Charlie Vosper knew him?'

'Yes, that's what. How did you guess?'

'I know my Inspector Vosper.' Paul grimaced and put the cup of cocoa on the floor to let the sediment settle. 'So what do we know about this man Walters?'

'Don't let that cocoa get cold, Temple. It seems that you were involved in the death of a girl called Bobbie Jameson a few days ago. Inspector Vosper has been conducting some routine enquiries, looking into her habits and background. Her boyfriend was Carl Walters.'

Paul was impressed. 'I like the way Charlie Vosper ties everything in so neatly. Did he say whether Walters has a record?'

Inspector Morgan shook his head. 'Not in this country he hasn't, although he might be known to the FBI. He's a bit of a corkscrew. He owns three amusement arcades down in London.'

'He sounds worth knowing,' Paul murmured thoughtfully. The woman police constable returned with a sledge-hammer. 'Excuse me, sir,' she said. 'This shouldn't take a moment.' And while Paul watched in astonishment she placed the safe in the centre of the floor. 'Stand back!' She stood over the safe, flexed her muscles and then swung the sledge-hammer in a mighty curve. The impact was deafening.

When Paul opened his eyes again he saw that the door of the safe had snapped at the hinges and was buckled inwards. The stone floor of the office appeared to be unharmed.

'Thank you, Jackson,' said the inspector. 'That seems to have done the trick, doesn't it?'

The woman winked at Paul. 'You have to know exactly where to bash it.' She left with the sledge-hammer over her shoulder.

'What,' asked the inspector, 'do we expect to find now, eh, Temple? Can I have your prediction?' He came from behind his desk and knelt beside the safe. 'Come along, man, you must have arrived at some tentative conclusions.'

'I can't imagine what we might find,' Paul said cautiously. 'Although I guess that Philip Baxter was involved in some shady business, and that was why he couldn't go to the police when his boys were in danger. In all probability it was a shady business that involves Lord Westerby.'

'And Carl Walters,' said the inspector, 'we mustn't forget him. The big time racketeers from London could very well be involved. Perhaps that was why Philip Baxter wanted to draw back. He may have thought the shady business was getting out of hand.'

'Very likely,' said Paul. He wished impatiently that the inspector would look inside the safe. 'But with any luck we shall soon know what it's all about.'

'What kind of rackets,' the inspector asked sceptically, 'do you think might be operated in the north riding of Yorkshire?'

'I don't know. What are the usual run of petty crimes?'

Inspector Morgan chuckled. 'You know what these folk are like. They sometimes get caught with their fishing-boats in somebody else's territorial waters. A century ago they used to do a spot of poaching, and some of them weren't above a little smuggling on the side. During the eighteenth century the villagers of Dulworth used to lure cargo vessels on to the rocks at night and steal from the wreckage. But these days they'd be the despair of any ambitious policeman. They don't even try to dodge paying their television licence fees.'

'The thing about Philip Baxter,' said Paul, 'is that he was a retired stockbroker. He wasn't your average Yorkshireman.'

'Ah, very true.'

Inspector Morgan tipped the safe on its side. There were several piles of burnt paper, which had probably been about twenty-five pounds in notes and some stocks. And there was a leather bound notebook. The leather was rigid and brittle from the fire, but it was still possible to read the notes inside.

'What is it?' Paul asked.

'I think it's in code. Columns and columns of figures, with a few dates and diagrams. I'll send it to Scotland Yard to be translated.' He looked up at Paul and grinned. 'Well, at least we know one thing. Mr Baxter hadn't retired. And if that cottage was destroyed to make sure that nobody found this notebook then I think we must be on to something.'

Paul nodded. 'Somebody is probably anxious to find this. Anxious enough to torture Philip Baxter and effectively kill him. I suppose you'll be calling in the Yard?'

'We'll see.' The inspector showed the usual reluctance to call outsiders in to solve a case and steal the glory. 'We'll wait and see what this notebook shows when it's been decoded. I'll send a man down to London with it tomorrow.'

'I'm going back tomorrow evening,' Paul said impulsively. 'I'll take it and hand it over personally to Charlie Vosper.'

The inspector thought for a few moments, and then agreed. 'All right, but I'll have the thing photocopied first. Call in sometime during the afternoon and I'll have it ready. Wrapped up and sealed.'

'Don't worry,' said Paul, 'you can trust me.'

Chapter Five

'Oh good,' Steve said excitedly, 'I love picnics. And it's such a glorious morning for it.' She loaded the hamper into the boot of the car. 'I know a superb spot beside a stream.'

'No. We're going along the cliffs,' said Paul. 'I prefer the sea and a spot of rock climbing to your endless Wuthering Heights.'

Steve watched him bring out a large first-aid box. There was something about this expedition that Paul hadn't admitted to. But Steve climbed into the car and enjoyed the illusion of being on holiday. She lapsed into memories of her own, spurred by the sight of a road or a house or a distant village to remember her childhood friends and excursions. She hoped desperately that in years to come she would still remember the pleasant early associations instead of the violence of these last few days.

She caught occasional glimpses of the picturesque little railway and realised that Paul was watching it carefully as well. Steve knew her husband well enough to guess what was in his mind. But she was damned if she was going to become involved again. She had watched Paul sit for an hour on the hotel veranda before they left. He had been smoking that odious pipe, which was a sure sign that he was solving a mystery or planning a novel.

The road swung inland and rose at a sharp gradient until the bay and Dulworth village were suddenly revealed low in the distance, spread out and glittering in the sunshine. The railway had vanished into the rock somewhere beneath them. Paul continued driving for another five minutes and then pulled into the side of the road.

'Shall we walk from here?' asked Paul.

A stray sheep had been chewing absent-mindedly at a gorse bush. It paused to watch them unload the hamper and the medicine box and rug, then bounded away as they set off for the cliff's edge. It wasn't accustomed to people.

'How far do you think we are from the village?' Paul asked with an elaborate air of unconcern. 'We don't want to bump into anyone we know. Might spoil our little treat.'

'We're three miles from the village,' Steve said precisely. 'The railway runs almost directly beneath us, with a sharp bend hereabouts, and it emerges from the tunnel somewhere over there, by that brown cliff face half a mile away.'

Paul looked surprised. 'Railway?' he said innocently. 'Oh, you mean the railway. Yes, I see.' He turned enthusiastically to look at the sea. 'A perfect spot, don't you think, darling? Let's stop here. I'm ravenously hungry!'

Steve laughed and spread out the rug. 'Yes, let's stop here.' As if she had any choice!

The hotel chef had packed a selection of pate, salad, shrimps, thin slices of smoked salmon and a quantity of tiny crisp rolls. There was carefully wrapped damp lettuce, a pile of thick turkey sandwiches, fruit and a bottle of Chateau Neuf du Pape 1959.

'Not a bad effort,' Paul said patronisingly. 'Do you approve?'

'Delicious,' Steve said with her mouth full. 'I shall sleep all the afternoon. In fact I'll stay here and sunbathe, if you'll remember to turn me over every half-hour.'

Paul poured a small quantity of wine into a disposable plastic cup. 'Will you taste it?' he asked. And when Steve had pronounced it perfect he filled the two cups. 'It's nice to get away from the all mod-con society, isn't it?' he murmured. 'I enjoy living rough, lighting fires with two sticks and eating the food that God has provided.' He bit into a turkey sandwich. 'I thought we might while away the afternoon with stories of piracy and smugglers. There are lots of caves along this stretch of the coast. Did you used to explore them as a child?'

'No,' said Steve, 'I didn't.'

'Oh.' Paul dangled his legs disappointedly over the cliff edge. 'What, none of them?'

'No, none.'

'Where was your sense of adventure?' He accidentally dropped a slice of turkey over the precipice. As he peered over to watch a seagull swoop on the meat something appeared to catch his attention. 'I say, darling, have you looked down here? It's all burned, as if there has been a fire. Looks rather bad.'

Steve peered over. The cliff was at least two hundred feet high, and a third of the way down the earth and the smattering of vegetation was scorched and battered. 'This must be where that aeroplane crashed,' she said.

'Good Lord, yes. I'd forgotten about that. We'll go exploring after lunch. I think we could manage this cliff face. There's a kind of goat track a hundred yards along—'

'I'm staying up here to sunbathe.'

Paul rolled over on to his back and put his head in Steve's lap. 'I've been thinking about young Draper's disappearance.

It seems to me that there are two possibilities.' He reached up, took Steve's sunglasses off her nose and put them on himself. 'Either he was put out of the train while they were still in the tunnel—'

'Or he was hidden somewhere on the train,' said Steve. 'The only snag about that deduction is that the police have searched the train and been all through the tunnel.'

'I thought we might have another look at the tunnel, especially at the bend where the train has to slow right down.'

Steve sighed. 'We'll finish our picnic first.'

By the time they had eaten their way through the feast and drunk the wine Steve was even more reluctant to give up an afternoon's sunbathing. But Paul tidied up the debris and took the hamper back to the car. He returned with a large torch.

'Come on,' he insisted, 'down we go.'

'What are we looking for?'

'A boy,' he said. 'Boys these days are probably much more adventurous than you were in your youth. The boys of St Gilbert's probably have a barbecue down on the beach every Founder's Day, and they'll know every inch of these caves.'

Steve climbed wearily to her feet. 'Do you think the caves link up with the railway tunnel?'

'That's what we mean to find out.'

Paul took her arm and led her to the goat track. They slithered down a perilous incline and then walked along a grassy stretch to the next sudden descent. The path wound easily and then dropped with a lurch, zig-zagging gradually lower, until slightly more than halfway down the cliff face they reached the first of the caves.

'This is as good a place as any to start,' said Paul.

Steve peered into the cave. 'I thought you were supposed to be visiting Miss Maxwell sometime today?'

'No particular time. I intended to pop out to her boat later this afternoon. When we've found John Draper.'

His voice echoed in the distance, which seemed to indicate that the cave extended well into the cliff. Paul shone the torch ahead of him. The walls were dry and almost smooth. After a few yards they had to crouch as they proceeded, but movement was easy. Generations of smugglers had ensured that the passage remained usable.

Paul felt that they ought to pass a few skeletons and relics of seventeenth century musket battles, but in fact the cave was clean and tidy. A Coca-Cola bottle where the ground sloped suddenly downwards, and a couple of cigarette ends where a courting couple had made love sometime in the past fifty years. There were marks in the dust where a crab or a badger had passed. Paul wondered what traces a badger would leave. Crabs leave parallel lines, like a railway track.

The passage forked about thirty feet in, and Paul listened for some indication of the better choice to take. He could hear only the hollow rolling of the sea. He clapped his hands, and a few seconds later the echo returned from the right fork. Paul took the left.

Paul was shining the torch on the walls and wondering idly why there were no hunting scenes as they have in French caves when Steve grabbed his arm. 'Careful!' she said nervously. 'There's a pot-hole in front of you.'

It led through to another cave ten feet below. Paul lowered Steve down the pot-hole and let her fall the last few feet, then he swung down after her. 'This is beginning to look promising,' he said. The torch revealed some small stalactites and stalagmites further in, and the cave quickly widened out into a cavern with several passages leading off. 'We ought to take this up as a hobby.'

Steve shivered. 'Couldn't we take up something warmer? I wanted to sunbathe this afternoon.'

The walls were damp and they could hear a minor waterfall in the distance. A low rumbling noise grew into the roar of an approaching train. Steve clung apprehensively to Paul's arm, half expecting the train to hurtle through the cavern itself, but then they heard it slow down and gradually vanish again through another tunnel.

'I think that was somewhere below us,' said Paul.

'Whereabouts below us?' Steve sounded as though she was regretting the whole picnic outing. 'Shouldn't we have left a trail of cotton back to the entrance? We'll probably be lost down here for days.'

Paul laughed. 'I have an infallible sense of direction.'

'So where's the sea?'

Paul gestured vaguely behind them. 'Somewhere over there.'

They had reached a fall of loose rock which extended sharply down about twenty feet. 'If we slither down there,' said Steve, 'we'll never get back.' She watched Paul descend to the floor of the next cave. 'Did you leave word with the hotel?' she asked, 'just in case we aren't back for dinner?'

'It's all right, darling, I told them we'd be out. We're dining with Lord Westerby.'

'That wasn't what I meant.'

Steve joined him more rapidly than she had intended, travelling the last few yards on her bottom. It wouldn't have mattered so much if Paul hadn't laughed. And if the ground wasn't so wet. They were obviously at sea level, and Steve wondered whether they would be drowned when the tide came in.

'Draper!!' Paul called. His voice came back at three different intervals. A rat scurried away, frightening Steve, splashing into an unseen stream. 'Are you here, Draper?'

'Why should he be here?' Steve demanded nervously.

Somewhere in the distance they heard a moaning noise.

'He's here all right,' said Paul. 'It was the only place he could possibly be.'

They waited until John Draper moaned again and then set off along the low passage. Beyond the next bend they saw him, lying exhausted and semi-conscious in a pool of water. He was crying, which Steve found for some reason more disturbing than if he had been hurt. He was crying like a frightened schoolboy who has spent two days lost in a labyrinth underground.

'Who did this to him?' Steve asked.

'Nobody. He did it to himself. He jumped the train when it slowed down at the bend,' said Paul. 'I thought that was obvious.'

They lifted the delirious boy to his feet and then began the long, laborious process of taking him back to the outside world.

'We'll send him home,' said Paul two hours later. 'He hasn't committed a crime.'

'But he's caused some confusion. Why did he jump the train?'

'He put two and two together,' said Paul. He looked down at the sleeping figure in the back of the car. 'Unfortunately, he made it add up to four. I think he was being too simple.' Paul smiled knowingly. 'Would you like to take him home? A decent meal and a good night's sleep and he should be back to normal. He's a resilient lad, and he's learnt his lesson.'

'What's that?' asked Steve.

'Crime,' Paul pronounced, as if it were a newly minted epigram, 'does not pay.'

Chapter Six

Paul Temple stood on the jetty and breathed deeply of the sea air. It was still a sweltering hot afternoon above ground, ideal for messing about in boats. For a few minutes he watched the leisured scene, people pottering about with fishing nets, touching up the paintwork on a scratched hull and loading trawlers with provisions. The calmly purposeful atmosphere was spoiled only by the gulls soaring and swooping overhead in a flurry of squabbles.

He wondered which of the boats lying at anchor in the bay was the *Windswept*. They were too far out to read. Half a dozen luxury yachts, perhaps four hundred yards from the shore. No sign of life on any of them.

'Afternoon, Mr Temple!' somebody called.

Tom Doyle's florid face was peering out of a hatch three boats along. He waved and then clambered ashore.

'What are you doing, Mr Temple?' he asked. 'Absorbing the local colour?'

'I was wondering how to get out there to a boat called *Windswept*. I have an appointment . . .' He waited until Tom Doyle had finished wiping his palms on an oily rag and then shook hands. 'I didn't realise everybody would be so busy this afternoon.'

'I'll row you out,' said Tom Doyle. 'Just hang on while I finish cleaning myself up.' He chuckled proudly. 'Been giving the old girl some fresh grease in her joints. She's growing old.'

'That's very kind of you,' said Paul. 'I'll wait.'

Tom Doyle replaced the flooring and put away the can of grease. 'Climb across into the dinghy,' he said. 'Careful.' He laughed as Paul lowered himself gingerly into the boat. 'That's it. We'll have you out to Lord Westerby's old tub within fifteen minutes.'

'Is it Lord Westerby's?' asked Paul.

'It was Lord Westerby's, though I believe Miss Maxwell runs it now. They say the old boy gave it her as a Christmas present.' He untied the mooring ropes and jumped aboard with casual familiarity, using the oars to push the rowing boat clear of his motor cruiser. 'Not that she actually runs it as such. She uses the yacht as a retreat more than anything else. Funny girl, Miss Maxwell. She writes poetry.'

The rowing boat was bucking slightly as it rode across the waves, but Tom Doyle pulled effortlessly into the bay, and as soon as they were fifty yards out from the shore the water settled into a swelling movement which Paul found quite restful. He even found the sea breeze a pleasantly cooling experience.

It seemed as if the *Windswept* was the newly painted blue and cream boat lying slightly north of the others. Tom Doyle glanced occasionally over his shoulder, explaining that the currents were strong in the bay, and moved towards it in an arc.

'What size crew would they need on a boat like that?' Paul asked him, 'assuming they were taking it out?'

'Well, when his Lordship had it there were two men and a boy. But I don't know whether they're still employed.'

'Local people?' Paul asked conversationally.

'No, sir. The boy was a foreigner. I don't know what he was, I'm sure. And the men came from Jersey.' Tom Doyle's face was creased with disapproval. 'They were a rum crowd. Kept very much to themselves. It used to be quite a bone of contention amongst the local people.' He paused in his rowing, spat on his hands, and resumed. 'We felt that his Lordship should have employed a local crew. Although I suppose he's in a position to please himself.'

Paul agreed. 'So Lord Westerby hasn't done much sailing this year?'

'Not as I've noticed. When his secretary wanted a bit of sea air I took him out in my old crate.' Tom Doyle laughed at the memory. 'That young Peter Malo, he's a character if you like! Have you met him?'

'Yes,' Paul admitted. 'Did he help you at all? With the fishing, I mean?'

'Help me? He damn nearly fell overboard every time he moved. Why the devil he came out with me I'll never know. The only time I had any peace was when he was peering through his binoculars, which he did for a couple of hours.'

'When was this?' Paul asked.

'Oh, about three weeks ago.'

They had come alongside *Windswept* and Tom Doyle drifted expertly to the rope ladder hanging over the side. 'This is it, Mr Temple. Do you want me to wait, or can I pick you up later?'

'That's very kind of you. I'd be glad if you could call back in about an hour.'

Paul climbed the rope ladder without much difficulty and when he reached the deck he swung himself on board feeling quite the seasoned mariner. He waved down at Tom Doyle and then set about finding the new owner.

'Miss Maxwell!' he called.

She was not on the sun-deck, which was where she ought to have been on an afternoon like this. She was probably in her cabin, Paul thought, typing out an Ode to a Seagull or a sonnet welcoming summer. 'Miss Maxwell!' Somehow he couldn't imagine it being a sensitive evocation of romantic love. She wasn't that sort of girl. But she wasn't below decks either.

Paul strolled on to the bridge and stood there like Captain Bligh scanning the sea for men overboard. 'Clap that man in irons, Mr Christian,' he said in an appalling imitation of Charles Laughton. 'Full steam ahead to Jamaica. Turn right at the lighthouse and keep going.' He wondered what Diana Maxwell did on board all day. Did she cultivate an obsession with white whales? He decided to read her poetry again. See whether she used the line, 'Better to reign in Hell than serve in Heaven.' He slid down to the deck, tucked an imaginary telescope under his arm and looked up at the sun. 'Five minutes to four,' he murmured.

'Hello, there!' somebody called. It was the voice of Diana Maxwell being carried on the breeze.

Paul peered over the side. 'Ahoy there,' he called cheerfully. 'You want to be careful of the sharks. Barry Fitzgerald lost a leg that way.'

She laughed and reached up for the rope ladder. 'I saw you come out, but I was having afternoon tea with Gerry Cazabon.' She gestured towards the next yacht a few hundred yards away. 'Sorry to keep you waiting.' With enviable athleticism she shinned up the ladder.

'Allow me,' said Paul, lending an unnecessary arm.

She was without a doubt a breath-taking girl. She paused on the rail of the boat, tossed her blonde hair loosely over her shoulders, and then seemed to freeze. It seemed to Paul that several seconds passed before he heard the gunshot. Then Diana Maxwell gasped and slumped forward on to the deck.

The first person to reach *Windswept* was Tom Doyle, five minutes after the shot and considerably out of breath. By that time Paul had established that the bullet had entered the girl's body under her left shoulder. She was still unconscious and Paul had left her exactly as she had fallen. He had torn up a sheet which he had used to stem the bleeding and keep the sun from her face.

Paul was staring uncertainly at the small radio transmitter when Tom Doyle called up, wondering whether to spend time trying to contact the coastguards or experiment with the engines until he could manoeuvre the boat single-handed into shore.

'Thank God you've come back,' said Paul. 'We have to get Miss Maxwell to a doctor.'

'I thought I heard a shot,' he said.

Tom Doyle was a good man in an emergency. He glanced at Diana Maxwell to confirm that it had been a shot, and wasted no time on the how or who of the situation. 'We'll try the engine,' he said. 'The sails will take too long, especially with this light breeze across the bay.' He disappeared briefly below, and while he was gone the engine spluttered into life. The yacht shuddered, and then continued a rhythmic trembling motion.

'Are we ready to cast off?' asked Paul.

'Aye.' Tom Doyle showed him how to put the engine in gear. 'Full steam ahead when I've raised the anchor,' he said, 'and be careful not to over steer. That's the choke, and you'll need to cut it out once we're away. Okay?'

Paul nodded. 'Can you work the radio, Tom?'

'Yes. I'll have a doctor waiting at the harbour.'

'You'd better notify the police as well.' He leaned out of the bridge. 'And if you can manage to get a message to Lord Westerby so much the better.'

The boat surged forward with a great swirling wash from the screws, cutting easily through the water, not at all like a rusty tub that hadn't been moved since Christmas.

Paul stood on deck and watched the ambulance drive away. She should live, Dr Stuart had hazarded, but an emergency operation was needed. The ambulance wound its way up the hill and vanished, leaving the participants in the drama feeling suddenly aimless.

'Damned grateful to you for acting so promptly, Temple,' said Lord Westerby. 'Lucky you were on the spot.'

'Thank Tom Doyle,' said Paul. He looked down at the part-time fisherman and odd job expert sitting on a bollard and rolling a cigarette. 'We were lucky Tom came back so fast.' He fell into step beside Lord Westerby and walked the length of the yacht before speaking again. 'I'm afraid,' he said at last, 'when somebody is determined to kill a girl then it's only a matter of time before he succeeds. I gather this is the fourth attempt to kill Miss Maxwell.'

'Where did the bullet come from?'

'Impossible to say. From the shore, perhaps, or one of the boats moored out there. I assumed it was the shore, but I wouldn't be certain.'

Lord Westerby was a big man and he concealed his emotions beneath a blustering and overbearing manner. He grunted impatiently at Paul's imprecision. 'What's this all about, Temple?' he demanded. 'Has the world gone mad? Why has this insane violence descended on Dulworth Bay?'

'I was hoping that you might tell me.'

Westerby snorted at the affront.

'Apparently you and a man called Walters paid a visit to Philip Baxter,' Paul persisted, 'the evening before the two boys went missing. I thought your visit might have been a key factor—'

'I do not know anybody called Walters.' Westerby paused in his perambulation of the deck to glare directly into Paul's face. 'I've already told Inspector Morgan that I've never met the man, and I am not in the habit of paying social calls on people like Baxter.'

Paul Temple murmured, 'I see,' and resumed the walk until he reached the gangplank. 'Oh well, I'm afraid I won't be taking up your invitation to dinner this evening, Lord Westerby. Business in London. But I'll be back. See you in a day or so.' He shook hands.

'Sorry not to have been more helpful,' said Lord Westerby.

Paul walked ruefully along the quayside. There were some men one didn't bother to argue with, and Lord Westerby was one of them. Exposing him for a liar would be the more sensible course. Paul sighed. The whole damned household was quite pig-headed. If Diana Maxwell had said what she had to say down in London . . . Paul stopped by the bollard.

'Tom! What are you waiting for?'

'Me, Mr Temple?' Tom Doyle threw his cigarette into the sea. 'I was just off. Plenty to do on a day like this, I can tell you.'

'Were you waiting to find out what Lord Westerby had said to me?' Paul asked suspiciously. 'Because he vehemently denies your whole story.'

'Aye,' Tom said fatalistically.

'Your story was true, wasn't it? His lordship did visit Baxter with this American?'

'Oh yes.' He nodded. 'I think so. Although I suppose I might have been mistaken.'

'How could you be mistaken? You've known Lord Westerby for years! It either was him or it wasn't.' Paul crouched in exasperation beside the man. 'When you made your statement you seemed pretty sure it was Westerby. You even said that Lord Westerby spoke to you.'

Doyle smiled apologetically. 'I know, Mr Temple, but now I come to think of it I do believe it was the other man who spoke to me.'

'Walters? But you said that Walters was a stranger. You'd never seen him before. So why should a complete stranger speak to you?'

'Why shouldn't he?' Doyle asked. 'I nodded politely and so he said good evening. That's common enough in these parts.'

'So when you arrived at the cottage that evening you saw Mr Baxter talking to this chap Walters and another man who *might have been* Lord Westerby?'

'That's right.'

'In fact,' Paul continued sarcastically, 'I suppose the more you think about it the more you realise that it probably wasn't Lord Westerby after all!'

Doyle glanced over his shoulder at the *Windswept*. Then he gave a petulant shrug. 'Yes, that's about it.'

'Tom, I don't think you've really considered the seriousness of your situation. Suppose the police decide that you didn't see Lord Westerby? They might also decide you were mistaken about the rest of your story. They might even decide that you never went near the Baxter cottage that evening, that your account of the kidnapping was an elaborate lie!'

'What do you mean?' Tom Doyle became anxious. 'Of course I went to the cottage. I saw Mr Baxter. That was when he told me about the boys! You must believe me, Mr Temple. I did see Mr Baxter.'

Paul smiled. 'I believe you, Tom. I believe everything you told the police, including that you saw Lord Westerby.' He stood up. 'My goodness, look at the time. I must be off.'

'I never saw— Hey, Mr Temple!'

'I'll see you when I get back from London!'

Paul left the man protesting on the quayside.

Chapter Seven

Halfway down the M1 they pulled in for supper at one of the motopian restaurants which straddle the motorway facing glassily in both directions. It was crowded as always, and Steve queued up for fifteen minutes to buy two cups of coffee and some sandwiches in cellophane wrappings.

'I thought we were having a meal,' said Paul.

'They only serve breakfast. Eggs, bacon, baked beans. I didn't think you'd fancy—'

'No, I don't. We should have turned off at Doncaster and found that little pub—'

'There isn't time. It'll be midnight before we reach London.'

Paul picked disconsolately at the ham sandwich, confirmed that he could tell margarine from butter no matter how thinly it was spread, and stirred his coffee. He watched the other diners in their open-necked shirts and holiday trousers, men unleashed from the office and factory for a fortnight and women freed from the shackles of home taking their children with them. Blackpool, here they come! Yet the air of pleasurable excitement was not contagious.

'I'm not very hungry,' Paul decided.

They had set off from Whitby just before six. Paul had called in at the police station to say goodbye and collect the package for delivery to Inspector Vosper. So far they were covering the three hundred miles in very good time.

'So let's go,' said Steve. 'I've never liked these places.'

A boozy coach party was straggling into the restaurant, singing 'You'll never walk alone' and shouting 'Up the north!' with great enthusiasm. Paul took Steve's arm and guided her through the confusion. They collided with an excitable little man who was operating a fruit machine by the entrance. A hail of tokens was gushing into the tray and he jumped back in ecstasy.

'Oh dear! Sorry, squire,' the man said quickly. 'Was that your foot?' He held Paul upright while they regained their balance. 'I don't usually win on these things. Are you okay?' He patted Paul on the back.

'Yes, that's all right.'

They went across the car park and found their car. Only another hundred and twenty miles to go. Paul followed a petrol tanker out into the filter lane to join the main stream of traffic. Suddenly he stamped on the brakes.

'What is it?' Steve demanded.

'I've had my pocket picked.' Paul opened his jacket and showed an empty inside breast pocket. 'My wallet's gone, and also the diary.'

'The man at the one-armed bandit,' said Steve.

Paul was trying to reverse into the car park again while two frantic drivers behind him hooted and gesticulated.

'There he is!' Steve called.

A red E-type Jaguar flashed past on the inside lane, and from the yellow lights it looked likely that it was being driven by the excitable little gambler. Paul decided to put his money on the Jaguar and sped off in pursuit.

'I've been a fool,' Paul said bitterly. 'I noticed that damned car following us on the A64 and I thought nothing of it. I wasn't expecting trouble until we reached London.'

The E-type was doing nearly a hundred miles an hour and it was all Paul could do to keep the car's tail lights in sight. He hoped that a police patrol might stop the thing, or that as they neared London the traffic flow would slow it down.

'Will you recognise him again?' he asked Steve.

'I think so. Tight curly hair, dark, sharp features, five feet five inches, early forties, well dressed.'

Paul nodded. 'And he uses cosmetics for men. Old Spice.'

'That seems to take care of him,' said Steve. 'So why don't we slow down? You could telephone Inspector Vosper and have the man picked up at Mill Hill.'

'Certainly not. Charlie Vosper would laugh at me.'

Paul pressed his foot down and watched the speedometer needle creep past the hundred mark. It was really rather dangerous, he realised, as a long-distance lorry pulled out in front of him and nearly forced him through the centre barrier. Paul overtook on the inside and then told Steve she could open her eyes again.

They were passing the Leicester service station when Paul drew abreast of the red E-type. The excitable man glanced over his shoulder and kept going. They were driving side by side towards a coach in the centre lane. Paul kept the E-type boxed in, so that the man would either have to slow down or hit the coach.

'Don't be a fool!' hissed Steve.

The E-type swung out in an effort to force Paul off the road, but then the man's nerve failed. He braked too quickly and swung back in across the motorway. His Jaguar seemed to go out of control and with a hideous screeching it spun on to the soft shoulder. Thirty faces watched in horror from the coach.

Paul came to a halt a hundred yards farther on and then ran back to the E-type. He found the excitable man staggering from his car in a state of near hysteria. 'Are you mad?' he shouted at Paul. 'Were you deliberately trying to kill me?'

'I was trying to stop you,' said Paul. 'I want that notebook back.'

'I don't know what you're—'

The man backed away from Paul in dismay. He tripped over the rear bumper and lay spreadeagled on the boot while Paul reached into his inside breast pocket. Paul found his wallet and the envelope containing the notebook exactly where he expected it to be.

'You squalid little man,' said Paul. 'What are you doing with these?'

The man looked likely to burst into tears. 'Well, we all have to make a living,' he bleated.

'What's your name?'

'They call me Lou the Dip.'

'You're lying!' Paul lifted him on to the back of the Jaguar. 'I've never met a common pickpocket who drives an E-type. Why did you steal this notebook?'

'I was after your wallet—'

Paul punched the man hard in the stomach, and as the man writhed sideways, thrust his head violently against the roof of the car.

'Now, I want to know who you're working for!'

'I'm a freelance—'

He broke off as Paul lifted him bodily into the air and threw him on to the edge of the motorway. The man struggled to his feet in terror only to find his arms gripped from behind. One sharp push from the rear would shoot him headlong on to the motorway.

'All right, all right,' he cried, 'I'll tell you. I was hired to knock off a leather-bound notebook. I don't know nothing else except—'

'Who hired you?'

'A man called Carl Walters. He said he'd pay me two hundred quid if I dipped it between Whitby and London, so I did. I mean, wouldn't you? It was easy money.' He sheepishly brushed the dirt off his clothes and adjusted the creases in his trousers. 'Or at least it should've been. I didn't know I'd be mixing it with a bloody professional. When a Mr Big gives you a job like that you don't ask too many questions, do you?'

Charlie Vosper listened to the story and then roared with laughter. 'Lou!' he said delightedly. 'Fancy you being taken by old Lou!' He laughed for several seconds, and then wiped the tears from his eyes. 'What's Lou doing these days? Is he making a living?'

'He's driving around in an E-type Jaguar,' Paul said sourly. 'And I wasn't taken by Lou Kenzell because the notebook is there in front of you.'

Vosper picked it up. 'We'll soon have it decoded, don't worry.' He grinned at Steve. 'I suppose you two have been too busy enjoying your holiday to devote much time to this Baxter business. But it's all right, I gather Inspector Morgan got the boys back. He seems to have everything under control.'

'What happens when he lets things get out of hand?' Steve demanded angrily.

'In Dulworth Bay?' He waved dismissively. 'Nothing ever happens in that part of the world. Bill Morgan's life is one long holiday. But while you lot have been swimming and sunning yourselves by the sea we've been pursuing our investigations at this end. We've been busy.'

'Oh yes?' enquired Paul. 'So who is the mysterious Curzon?'

'Ah, yes, Curzon.' He sniffed thoughtfully. 'I wonder. Do you fancy Carl Walters, or is your money on Lord Westerby?'

'I'm pretty damned sure that Curzon is—' But Paul stopped himself in time. No point in showing off simply because Charlie Vosper was enjoying himself. 'No, I can't commit myself until I know more about Carl Walters. I'd like to meet him first.'

Vosper nodded his encouragement. 'Yes, good idea. You have a chat with him, Temple. He might reveal something in the odd unguarded moment, confess by some slip of the tongue to killing his girl-friend and Philip Baxter. He won't admit it to us thick headed policemen, but you might manage to trip him up. I mean, being as how you're a friend of the assistant bloody commissioner.'

'True,' Paul said serenely. 'Where do I find this guileless American?'

'At the Octagon gallery. He owns it.'

'I was thinking,' Steve intervened diplomatically, 'that I might trip him up. I know the police are thorough and my husband writes excellent books, but the feminine approach sometimes has its advantages. After all, I'm not constrained by the Judges' Rules, am I?'

'Do you know what the Octagon gallery is?' Vosper asked sourly. 'Do you know its reputation?'

Steve laughed. 'Of course I know the Octagon, it's a thriving new commercial gallery just off Bond Street.'

'It's a front,' said Vosper, 'a front, you take my word for it.'

*

It was many years since Steve had been an art student, but she enjoyed dressing the part again. She put on an old pair of blue denim jeans with frilly bottoms, one of Paul's white shirts, open sandals and a rainbow coloured poncho. The total effect, she told herself, was very casual. She brushed her hair down over her shoulders and used a dead pan make-up with plenty of mascara round the eyes. It was nice to be young again. A few beads and bangles and she was ready to go.

Luckily Paul was out when the transformation was made, having an early evening drink with a stockbroker friend. She had the face and figure to carry such youthfulness, Steve decided, but she didn't want everybody to see her.

'Hey, you!' Kate Balfour shouted as Steve hurried down the stairs. 'Where do you think you're going?'

Steve stopped guiltily. 'I was just off to the Octagon.'

'Steve!' Kate Balfour hurried apologetically from the kitchen. 'I'm sorry, Steve, I thought you were a housebreaker. I didn't recognise you without a bra.'

'I don't think young people are wearing them these days.'

'Young people may not be,' she said enigmatically.

Steve fled, leaving the housekeeper muttering darkly about the youth of today, sex and permissiveness.

The Octagon had opened about a year ago with a flourish of pop people publicity. It was trendy and colourful, its previews were always good for a centre page spread of photographs and the kind of zany gossip stories that confirmed several million readers over breakfast in their opinion that all art was bunk. The Octagon had apparently prospered, attracting several important New York artists and finding several new English ones.

Steve arrived by taxi at half past seven. Two telephone calls had established that tonight a private view was being held of work by Ed Suleiman and that an invitation would be waiting for her at the door. But in fact Steve simply walked straight in and joined the throng. A man in the foyer said how lovely to see her and somebody else thrust a glass in her hand.

For a man who had made his money out of amusement arcades Steve had to admit that Carl Walters had created an impressive gallery. All the critics were there looking aloofly critical and several big collectors were looking nervously noncommittal. Ed Suleiman was the bearded man with the loud voice and he was telling the world what he thought of galleries.

'They should be burnt to the ground,' he was declaiming. 'They imprison paintings. Galleries are for businessmen, like banks.' He seemed to be against paintings as well, which encouraged the dealers to buy his work while they had the chance.

Steve joined a group of people who were discussing environmental art. She knew one of the girls from her college days and they went through the 'whatever happened to so-and-so' routine. Steve found that they had both lost touch with nearly everybody. All their old friends had married and disappeared into darkest Dorset, Norfolk and Golders Green.

'And what do you do now?' the girl asked.

'I design,' Steve pronounced. 'I gave up painting years ago.'

Ed Suleiman heard the remark and recognised a soul sister. He put a massive arm round her shoulder and continued to inform the world what he thought of people who bought paintings. Steve was one move closer to Carl Walters.

She took Carl Walters to be the tall and rather elegant man who was watching over the proceedings from the foot of the stairs. He was carefully groomed and expensively dressed.

His air of sardonic detachment was typical, Steve thought, of a man who knows how to manipulate the gallery system. He didn't look like a criminal.

'What do you think of my work?' Ed Suleiman asked in sudden challenge, as though he was wondering what his arm was doing round this strange girl.

Steve thought quickly. 'Terribly direct, bold and assertive,' she said, trying not to sound too glib. 'Your sense of form is a little reckless, but usually it works, doesn't it?'

Ed Suleiman nodded doubtfully. 'Yeah, sometimes. But it's all wallpaper.'

'I expect Michelangelo thought that sometimes about his work.'

'Well, he was right. Ceiling paper. What's your name?'

Steve glanced across the gallery to see where her old college friend had got to. 'Caroline Fawcett-Blake,' she said. 'I was invited because—'

'I like your bone structure. Fine and very stubborn. Your skin stretches over the cheeks with a nice effect.'

'Thank you.'

'What sort of hips are under all this gear?'

'Rather wide, I'm afraid—'

'That's how women are built. That's good. I like a fine, clean structure, without a lot of flesh slopping about on women to spoil the form. Caroline, eh?'

'Yes,' said Steve.

'My name's Ed. You must come back to my place after this circus is over. I'm throwing a small, private party, just you and me and Carl and a few friends.'

'Carl?'

'He's the man who owns the shop. Haven't you met him?' Ed Suleiman led her across to the man at the foot of the stairs. 'Hey, Carl,' he shouted, 'look who I've found! Bone structure like a pre-Raphaelite!'

Carl Walters had charm, Steve found. He managed to suggest that he and Steve were sharing the joke about her build to indulge the wayward artist. And he knew his art scene. He knew several of Steve's past tutors and could talk about them with amused familiarity. Steve had to make a real effort to remember that a man who was a connoisseur of painting could also be a villain.

'I haven't seen you before at my gallery,' he said when Ed Suleiman had gone off to tell one of the larger female guests that she had a body like a Renoir model. 'There must be something wrong with my publicity.'

'I spend a great deal of my time outside London. I'm a designer and I prefer to work in the country. I've a cottage near Broadway.'

'Beautiful spot,' murmured Walters.

They sat on the stairs and talked about design while the man who had welcomed Steve so effusively sold eight paintings at several hundred guineas each. Ed Suleiman and two rather drunken critics were shouting loudly in dispute over the relative qualities of Walt Disney and the cartoons featuring Tom and Jerry. It sounded as though the verdict went to Tom and Jerry. When that was settled Ed Suleiman went off in pursuit of a girl who was absolutely God-damned classical in her proportions.

'He asked me to go to his party,' Steve said laughing. 'But I think it might be a little crowded by the time he's finished.'

'You must come,' Walters insisted. 'They're always such noisy, boozy affairs; I need somebody civilised to talk to.'

'All right, but you'll have to take me. I came by taxi.'

'But of course.'

The preview ended when Ed Suleiman decided to go. He led a crowd of people out of the gallery with shouts of, 'Come on, everybody, the party's at my place! You're all invited!' And everybody seemed intent on going to it, except for the two rather drunken critics who were helped out to a taxi. Steve remained behind while Carl Walters supervised the locking up.

'So you come from Broadway?' he said as they watched the effusive young man putting the cheques in the safe.

'No, that's only where I live. I come from a place in Yorkshire that nobody's ever heard of. It's a tiny fishing village called Dulworth Bay.'

'Dulworth Bay?' he repeated in astonishment. 'Sure I know Dulworth Bay! I've got a whole heap of friends up there. Do you know Doc Stuart?'

'Yes, of course. Who doesn't in Dulworth Bay?'

Carl Walters laughed delightedly. 'Well, what do you know? And how about the big noise? Is he a friend of yours?'

'Lord Westerby? He's an old crony of daddy's. Don't you think he's a sweet old thing?'

'Not exactly. Lord Westerby and I aren't on visiting terms. He's a snob.'

'But frightfully rich.'

'Don't you believe it,' Carl Walters said contemptuously. 'He doesn't have a nickel to call his own.'

'Do you know the Baxters?'

'The Baxters? No, I don't think so. But then I never met you either, did I?' The young man was turning out the lights and preparing to set the alarms. 'I saw old Doc Stuart a fortnight ago when I was in Dulworth and he said that all the young people are leaving the district to come to London. I suppose you're a case in point. Will you wait for me? I must do a tour of the premises before we leave.'

Steve smiled her assent. 'Perhaps I could make a telephone call while I wait? Just to tell my flatmate I shan't be back until later.'

Walters left her in the office while he disappeared along the corridor. Steve dialled her home. 'Hello, Paul?' she whispered excitedly. 'This is Caroline Fawcett-Blake. I'm at the Octagon gallery with Carl Walters. I can't say much—'

'The Octagon?' From his voice Paul was obviously alarmed. 'Steve, what is all this nonsense? You don't know anybody called Caroline Fawcett-Blake! Do you realise the danger you're in? Stay where you are—'

'Sorry, darling, but I'm just off. Walters is taking me to a party. There's a mad artist who wants to show us his private collection of Tom and Jerry films.'

There was a horrified pause at the other end of the line. 'I won't hear of it. Steve, come home at once.'

'Sorry, darling, but I'm doing terribly well. And Carl is absolutely charming. He knows Dulworth Bay and we have lots of people in common. Don't worry.'

Steve replaced the receiver just as Carl Walters returned. He grinned, took Steve's arm and led her through a side door into the street. His gleaming Jensen was parked in a kind of delivery bay.

'What a super car!' Steve cooed.

'Not bad,' he said proudly. To demonstrate the Jensen's paces he accelerated to fifty miles an hour into Piccadilly and sped round Hyde Park Corner as if it were open country. The traffic trying to go into Hyde Park hooted angrily.

'How are the brakes?' Steve asked mildly.

'I never use them,' he said with a laugh, 'except when I see a police car. All the other cars on the road are fitted with brakes, aren't they?'

'I suppose so. You remind me of Diana Maxwell. She drives exactly like this. Except that her car is in the scrap yard.'

'Diana Maxwell? Ah yes, Lord Westerby's niece, or more likely his girlfriend. She's a first-class pain in the neck. If I were an English aristocrat I'd find a better mistress than the icy Miss Maxwell.'

They were hurtling along Knightsbridge. 'Where does Ed Suleiman live?' Steve asked.

'In Hampstead.'

Steve turned to him in surprise. 'But we should be going in precisely the opposite direction. Hampstead is north—'

'We aren't going to Hampstead,' said Carl Walters.

'So where are we going?'

'I'll give you three guesses, Mrs Temple.'

Steve suppressed a sudden feeling of panic. 'Oh,' she said softly, 'so you know.'

Carl Walters nodded. 'That telephone call of yours was a silly mistake.'

'Where are you taking me?'

The streets of London were suddenly blurred, although this might have been something to do with the speed at which they were travelling. Steve thought she noticed Kensington station, and later there was a bookshop she should have recognised. Darkness had settled and the street lighting mingled with the gaudy shop window illuminations to create a dazzling effect. The flicker of car lights turning left and right, the gleam of red brake lights and the changing spectrum of traffic lights all combined in a kaleidoscope of confusion.

'Stop this car!' she demanded. 'Do you hear? I insist that you stop this car!'

Walters laughed easily. 'Don't get excited, Mrs Temple. You'll find out where I'm taking you, when we arrive.'

Steve contemplated grabbing the steering wheel and sending the car at a lamp-post. Or jumping out at the next set of traffic lights, except that Walters had already gone through two sets of red lights. Something had to be done quickly. Once they were on to the A4 she would be lost.

'It was a clever idea of yours,' Carl Walters said cheerfully. 'A whole lot brighter than the police force's heavy footed activities. I've had CID to see me twice, the vice squad once and the drugs squad once. I'm expecting the traffic cops to pinch me for parking tomorrow.' He laughed. 'They haven't the faintest idea what they're after. All they know is that I must have done it.'

'Done what?'

'That, Mrs Temple, is the question.'

Steve tried to compose her mind by concentrating on the abstract problems of the case. Drugs squad, Walters had said. She wondered whether drugs were the key to the mystery. The art scene, with its roots in student life and tentacles reaching into all levels of society, was an ideal front for a man like Walters. Steve felt suddenly angry with herself for bungling the evening. A visit to Ed Suleiman's party would soon have confirmed her theory.

'If I'm not home by ten o'clock my husband will know where to find me,' she snapped.

Gradually the car slowed down. Steve reached surreptitiously for the door handle. They were cruising round one of those indistinguishable London squares, and this would be the finest opportunity she could expect for throwing herself on to the pavement. At the next corner . . .

Then she recognised where she was. 'But you've brought me home,' she said in amazement. Carl Walters had turned smoothly into the mews and was stopping at her front door. 'This is where I live.'

'Isn't this what you wanted?'

'Well, yes, but—' Steve climbed from the car feeling very relieved and a little deflated. 'I thought—'

'I know what you thought, honey. Perhaps some other time, eh?' He laughed uproariously as he reversed the car out of the mews and drove away.

Chapter Eight

'Dr Stern has amassed such a quantity of evidence in his book that there is no room left for the obvious conclusions. In a lengthy section on petty theft, for instance, the worthy doctor arrives at the scarcely surprising but tentative theory that one contributing factor might be poverty. In the subsequent seventeen pages Dr Stern considers the use of electric shock therapy, punitive detention, motivational redirection, but never does he consider giving the petty thief a little money to cure the poverty.'

The rattle of the typewriter ceased and Paul Temple read over what he had written. There, that was telling them. He smiled and poured himself another whisky. He was enjoying himself; he wasn't brooding on any of Steve's idiotic adventures!

'This is, of course, a misleading study because it does not place crime in any context of honesty. What is an honest man, and why? Is there a significant correlation between honesty and conformity and passivity? Does an honest man from an anti-social background need to be psychopathic and is it, furthermore, desirable to cure him? Or should he simply be removed to a group whose norms he can easily conform to?

None of these important and essential questions is considered in this superficial and one-sided book . . .'

The doorbell rang to interrupt the flight of fancy. Paul swore under his breath. It couldn't be Steve, because she had a key. It was always the way, when she was out and Kate Balfour had gone home, a stream of encyclopaedia salesmen came to disturb him.

'One wonders for whom such a book as this is intended—'

The damned bell rang again. Perhaps it was a policeman with news that Steve had – Rubbish! Paul continued typing.

'Certainly not the practising criminologist—'

He heard Steve's voice on the stairs and sprang to his feet. Thank God! She was prattling breathlessly to someone about how long he or she had been waiting and the fact that Paul had been home when she rang fifteen minutes ago. As though nothing had happened! Paul sat down again to work. He was damned if he'd show excitement or relief. He didn't care whether Carl Walters' collection of etchings was unique in this country. Steve had behaved in a foolhardy way. And besides, Paul was busy. He did like to deliver his copy on time, and for this review the editor had already rung up twice. The weekly magazine was due on the streets on Friday.

'Darling! Sir Graham said you must be out.' She hurried across the room to his desk and kissed him. 'Guess who's here!'

'Sir Graham?'

It was. Paul decided to give up gracefully and left his typewriter. He poured them both drinks and asked Steve why she was back so early.

'Well,' she said, 'actually, things didn't go too well. He overheard my telephone call to you.'

At least Steve's account of the evening was funny. Paul roared with rather malicious laughter, and even Sir Graham grinned.

'I must tell Charlie Vosper about this, Steve,' the assistant commissioner said unkindly. 'It will console him for my gaffe in discussing the case with you both at the party. Vosper hasn't forgiven me for that, but now he might.' He patted Steve on the shoulder and strolled across to Paul's desk. 'Charlie Vosper enjoys a good joke.' He peered inquisitively at the paper in the machine.

'That'll teach you,' Paul said complacently, 'to go to parties with strange men.'

'But darling, I think we're on to something now. I think we can assume this whole case is about drugs, don't you? They must be smuggling the drugs into Dulworth – smuggling is part of their traditional way of life up there – and bringing them down to London for distribution. I think Carl Walters is the distribution boss, operating from the Octagon or one of his other premises. He's too rich to have made his money legitimately.' She waved her glass at Sir Graham Forbes. 'Drugs, you see? That's why Baxter was so anxious to get out.'

Paul shrugged. 'That may be so. It doesn't much matter what the commodity is.'

'Doesn't matter? So why have I been risking a fate worse than death this evening?'

'I don't know.' Paul sat on the sofa beside her. 'Why have you been risking a fate worse than death?

'I hate you!'

Sir Graham Forbes looked up from the typewriter in surprise. 'I say, Paul, this is a bit severe. Won't Dr Stern sue you for libel? You can't dismiss his book as light bedside reading for the crossword puzzle addict.'

'He hasn't even read the book,' said Steve.

Paul pointed to the book open on the desk. 'There you are, I'm a fast reader. And I have a great respect for crossword puzzle addicts. Some of the more discriminating ones are readers of my own books, so I'm told by Scott Reed, and I never doubt the word of my publisher.'

Steve looked suspiciously at the whisky bottle. 'Paul, how much of that have you drunk already this evening? Too much whisky always makes you flippant. I'd have hidden the bottle if I'd known Sir Graham was coming.'

'Steve!' the assistant commissioner remonstrated. 'I may be a retired major general but I can hold my liquor!'

'Whenever you two settle down for an evening's gossip you finish the bottle and then discuss vintage Cagney films. Paul had a bruise for a week where he demonstrated that fall down the church steps with three bullets in his stomach—'

'*The Roaring Twenties*,' Paul explained. 'But that gives me an idea. Do you think I could accuse Dr Stern of an attitude towards crime based on seeing too many gangster films? His chapter on peer groups is straight out of *Angels with Dirty Faces*, where the Dead End Kids refuse to join the youth club—'

'And Cagney pretends to be yellow when he goes to the chair!' said Sir Graham enthusiastically.

'Oh shut up!' said Steve. 'I wish I'd spent the evening with Carl Walters. He would have told me all we want to know about the Curzon business.'

'I doubt it,' Paul said disparagingly. 'He doesn't know himself all that we want to know.' But he leaned over the armchair and kissed her on the top of the head. 'Never mind, darling, you didn't do so badly. You're still alive.'

'I did very well! Until Carl Walters discovered who I was he told me the truth. We know he's in the habit of visiting Dulworth Bay, that he's a friend of Dr Stuart. Did I tell you what he said about Diana Maxwell?'

'Yes, you did.'

'He said she was Lord Westerby's mistress.'

'But we still don't know Curzon's racket,' said Sir Graham.

Steve smiled ironically. 'That isn't important, Sir Graham. What matters is where, who and how. Something obviously went wrong when Baxter decided to get out, and I think I can guess what went wrong. Baxter decided to blackmail the rest of the gang. He had evidence in that notebook which would put them all in gaol for years.' She leaned forward in her chair. 'I suppose your code-breakers haven't found what the evidence is yet?'

'Good lord, I knew I had some reason for coming here. Yes–'

'You came,' Paul intruded, 'to lend me a copy of the report on that air crash.'

'Yes, but I've had word from Major Browning about the notebook. He spent all day going through those figures trying to find some meaning. There seemed to be absolutely no correlation between the numbers or sequences of numbers and any literal sense. Then just as he was going home this evening it occurred to him that the figures might be precisely what they appear to be, and that's what they are. Simply figures.'

'Figures referring to what?' asked Paul. 'Money, times, share index movements?'

Sir Graham shrugged his square-set shoulders. 'They appear to refer to measurements, a distance from some given object. But as we don't know what the given object is we are rather stymied.'

'A location,' Steve said thoughtfully, 'like the whereabouts of smugglers' treasure.'

Sir Graham Forbes took a file containing reports on the Dulworth Bay air disaster from his briefcase and left them on the desk with a warning not to tell Charlie Vosper where it came from. 'That man makes my life hell when he's upset,' said Sir Graham. 'He becomes withdrawn and formal and only speaks when he's spoken to. He's worse than my wife . . .' The thought clearly disturbed him, and he accepted another whisky to soothe his nerves. The myth of James Cagney had appealed to him, he said, because Cagney always had an answer to police inspectors, when he wasn't crushing grapefruits in women's faces.

'You're just a couple of overgrown schoolboys,' said Steve when they were in bed. She slithered down between the sheets, yawned, and snuggled against Paul. 'With every glass of whisky Sir Graham became more and more reactionary, and you encouraged him.' She giggled. 'I think Sir Graham is terribly sweet, but I don't understand how he became an assistant commissioner of police in this day and age.'

'He's damned good at his job,' said Paul. 'And after they'd taken away his colonial regiment naturally they had to find something for him to do. Otherwise he'd have gone into politics.'

Paul opened the file and propped it against his knees. He had enjoyed the evening; conversation had ranged euphorically from the cinema to literature to Sir Graham's slightly peppery views on society. They had been laughing a lot, and it required an effort of adjustment for Paul to turn his mind back to the Curzon case.

He studied the file. It had been a small private charter plane, en route to New York via Manchester for Amsterdam.

There had been only forty-six passengers, and they had all died instantly. American tourists, several civil servants, a trio of Dutch schoolteachers, a few businessmen and someone called Duprez. Duprez?

'What,' asked Steve suddenly, 'makes you so sure this air crash has anything to do with Curzon?'

'I'm not so sure. But the time factor interests me. It was after the plane crash that things began to go wrong with Baxter. That was when Peter Malo went sailing with Tom Doyle and a pair of binoculars, and then the boys disappeared. Carl Walters was in Dulworth. I don't approve of coincidence.'

Duprez was a mystery. The airline apparently knew nothing about him except that he was French and had booked as far as Manchester. The French police had not been able to contact any relatives and there had been no enquiries about him. A note in the file mentioned an impression formed by the customs officer at Schiphol that the man was something to do with the motor industry, but the impression could not be substantiated. All papers and documents had been destroyed when the plane caught fire on the cliffs.

So that didn't help Paul very much. If Duprez were a contact between the continent and Curzon's organisation it was obviously a false name, and now he was dead.

'What happens now?' asked Steve.

'I don't know.' Paul turned out the bedside lamp and stared into the darkness. No help from the report, no help from the notebook. 'I suppose we must tackle Carl Walters—'

'Tackle Walters?' Steve said indignantly. 'What the devil do you think I was doing this evening?'

'Risking a fate worse than death.'

When Paul telephoned next morning Carl Walters readily agreed to meet him. 'Yeah, sure,' he said. 'I had the pleasure yesterday of meeting your charming wife. Bring her along as well.'

'She'd be delighted,' Paul said bitterly. 'How about lunch at the Savoy grille?'

'Okay, why not? By the way, can you tell me what all the cloak and dagger stuff is about?'

'It's about a friend of yours called Lou. He says you hired him to steal a notebook from me.'

'Never heard of him. What sort of notebook is this?'

'A lot of measurements. You know, X marks the spot.'

Walters laughed and said that he didn't know what the hell was going on. But he'd see Paul for lunch at one o'clock.

At a quarter past one Carl Walters had not turned up. Paul ordered two more sherries and tried to suppress the desire for lunch.

'Did I tell you about my meeting with Jimmy Forester-Ford yesterday?' he asked Steve.

A look of instant boredom descended on Steve. 'No,' she said. 'Did he tell you to sell your *Imps* and buy *Canpacs*? Oh look, I'm sure that girl was on the cover of *Vogue* last month.'

'We were discussing Baxter most of the time. I wanted to know what his reputation was. Whether he'd ever been drummed out of the Stock Exchange, that sort of thing.'

'I suppose,' Steve said abstractedly, 'his word was his bond?'

'Well, yes, but he wasn't very highly regarded. Jimmy said that he didn't consider Philip Baxter a gentleman. He played the market like a gambler and made a fortune in the early days of the takeover boom, before the Stock Exchange drew up its rules to stop the kind of practices which Philip Baxter helped to invent.'

Steve nodded. 'In other words, Philip Baxter was none too scrupulous.'

'None too,' Paul agreed.

Someone was waving from the other side of the dining-room. Waiters moved aside in alarm as Kate Balfour pushed between the tables to reach them. She was out of breath and slightly flushed. 'I'm sorry it took me so long,' she gasped, 'but the traffic is awful. I came as soon as I got your message.'

'Message?' said Steve. 'I thought perhaps you'd come for the food.'

'What message was this?' asked Paul. 'We haven't—'

'A man telephoned to say that you wanted to see me here, urgently. Said he was the head waiter.' Kate looked bewildered. 'Was it a joke then?'

'No,' Paul said thoughtfully, 'No, it isn't a joke, Kate. Someone knew that we were here and they wanted to get you out of the flat. At this very moment I expect we have visitors.'

The flat had been, in police terminology, well turned over. Steve gasped in horror at the sight. The drawers were all pulled out and their contents had been tipped on the floor, the books had been tipped off the shelves, pictures had been thrust aside, furniture moved and the carpet disturbed. The search had been thorough in the living-room and the study. Steve ran off upstairs to see the damage to the bedroom.

'I suppose he was looking for the notebook,' Paul said bleakly.

Kate Balfour stared at the mess in the kitchen. 'Was it that man you were meeting at the Savoy?'

'Carl Walters? He certainly knew we'd be out, didn't he?'

'I'll give him hell if I lay hands on him!'

Paul went upstairs in search of his wife. The side effect of such housebreakings, Paul knew, was that women took them symbolically as a violation of their domesticity. Steve might be distressed.

She was sitting in the middle of the bedroom surrounded by a pile of clothes which had been roughly thrown from the wardrobe and the cupboards. There were cosmetics and jewellery strewn across the dressing-table. 'It'll take hours,' she said unhappily, 'to sort these out again.'

'Is there anything missing?'

'No. I don't think so.'

'Mr Temple! Here, quickly!' Kate Balfour had continued from room to room, and her voice came from the bath-room. 'Look who we've found.' She poked her head out and waved agitatedly.

It was Carl Walters, lying on the floor in a pool of his own blood, half unconscious and moaning to himself. Paul knelt beside the man, but there wasn't much he could do.

'I'm Paul Temple. Lie still and we'll call a doctor.' He nodded to Mrs Balfour. 'Will you, Kate?'

She looked as if she wanted to stay and tick the man off for being in the flat and making a mess of her kitchen, but another fit of coughing from Walters sent her hurrying downstairs.

'Who did this to you?' Paul asked gently.

'Don't move me,' he whimpered, 'leave me alone. God, it hurts!'

'I'll fetch some brandy,' said Steve.

Paul loosened the man's collar and made him comfortable. There was a strange smell of perfume in the room which somehow didn't tie in with Paul's image of the dying man. Paul put the oddity to the back of his mind; he would worry about peculiar smells when there was more time.

'You must tell me who did this,' Paul insisted. 'I know you were searching my flat to find the notebook. But somebody interrupted you, didn't he?'

Walters nodded. 'Temple,' he said, nearly inaudibly, 'You've got to stop Curzon getting the diamonds. Don't let him—' Suddenly his voice was lost.

When Steve returned with the brandy Paul drank it himself.

'Why should they turn your flat over, Temple? We've got the notebook down at the station. Why didn't they come and turn over my office?' Charlie Vosper fulminated for several minutes to establish that friends of Sir Graham Forbes were as nothing to him. 'What was the idea of meeting Carl Walters at the Savoy anyway?'

'I wanted to find out what this case was about.'

'So now you know,' the inspector said heavily. 'It's about diamonds.'

'I know.'

Steve brought in a tray of tea and toasted scones, which worked a minor improvement on the policeman. He almost smiled. He ate three scones while he was sitting at Paul's desk reading the sheet of paper in the typewriter. Then he grinned. 'That'll make Professor Stein stick to his lunatics, won't it? I don't understand a word of it, but I'm sure it's very amusing.'

They were taking Carl Walters away, and Steve stood by the door and watched him pass. 'Poor man,' she murmured. 'I rather took to him, you know. He had a smooth mid-Atlantic façade and lots of charm, but underneath it he was a rather nice man. He enjoyed his life.'

'He was a gangster,' said Charlie Vosper. 'I wouldn't be surprised if some of his boys didn't shoot that girl in the pub – you know, Bobbie Jameson. He had quite an organisation. What I don't understand is why he was doing your flat over himself. He should have got Joe to do it, or Lou Kenzell even, if that story about Lou working for him was true.'

Paul sipped his tea. 'Walters said he'd never heard of Lou.' Something in the back of Paul's mind was stirring to connect. Lou Kenzell, he said to himself, Lou Kenzell. What was it?

'Carl Walters wouldn't have had his own girl-friend shot,' said Steve. 'That's ridiculous. Carl Walters was obviously working on the other side, against our mysterious friend Curzon. That's why he's dead.'

'Perhaps,' said Vosper. 'Perhaps he was on Baxter's side.'

'Lou Kenzell!' Paul said suddenly. 'Of course, that's who it was, Lou Kenzell! He came here to search the flat for the notebook and he found Carl Walters already on the job. I couldn't place the smell, but I remember now—'

'What smell?' asked Steve.

'Old Spice. There was a strong smell of Old Spice in the bathroom.' He turned to Inspector Vosper. 'That was the first thing I noticed about Lou Kenzell when we encountered him on the motorway.'

Vosper was sceptical. 'Do you seriously expect me to pull him in on that kind of evidence?'

'Yes.'

Vosper picked up the telephone and dialled New Scotland Yard. He gave instructions that Lou Kenzell should be brought in for questioning and warned that he might be dangerous. 'I'll be in my office in half an hour,' he concluded, 'and I want Kenzell there waiting for me.' He hung up, finished his cup of tea and picked up another scone. 'Are you coming along, Temple? I'll need a statement from you anyway.'

Paul went along.

They found Lou Kenzell sitting in the police station with a policeman either side of him. He was contriving to look outraged, but he was obviously agitated. Vosper sniffed fastidiously and nodded to Paul. 'I see what you mean.'

Kenzell had sprung to his feet as the inspector came into the office, he demanded an explanation, but when he saw Paul Temple he subsided into his chair.

'What am I supposed to have done now?' he asked morosely.

A police sergeant sat at a desk in the corner of the room with a pencil poised above his notebook. Vosper made the man turn out his pockets. The tension was almost physical, Paul could sense it even with his back to the scene as he looked out of the window.

'If you think you can get me for picking your pocket, Mr Temple, it's not on,' he said desperately.

'You lied to me about that, Lou. You said that Carl Walters had hired you, and it wasn't true. Carl Walters denied your whole story.'

'Well, he would, wouldn't he? I mean, that—'

'Where,' Inspector Vosper cut in, 'were you this afternoon at half past one?'

'I want to ring my lawyer.'

'I don't like liars, Lou. You were told to steal that notebook by Curzon, weren't you? And Curzon said that if you were unlucky enough to be caught you should say you'd been hired by Carl Walters. Isn't that so?'

'I'm not saying anything.'

Inspector Vosper was a big man with very wide shoulders and he weighed fifteen stone. He loomed over Kenzell as if he would swallow him in one gulp. 'Louis Joseph Kenzell, you are not obliged to say anything, but I must warn you that anything you do say will be taken down and may be used in evidence.' The inspector returned to his chair behind the mahogany desk. 'Now, where were you at half past one this afternoon? We know you weren't at your flat—'

'There's no law against going to the pictures, is there?'

'None at all.' Charlie Vosper called across to the sergeant. 'Did you get that answer, Simpson? He replied, at half past one I entered Mr Temple's flat in order to steal a black leather bound notebook, and there I encountered the aforesaid Carl Walters—'

'Hey, that's bloody lies!' said Kenzell indignantly. 'I was at the pictures, and nobody aforesaid anything about Carl Walters being there.'

'Write that down, Simpson. A scuffle ensued between Walters and myself, at the height of which I lost control. I brought his head into heavy and deliberate contact with the wash-basin, thus rendering him unconscious, whereupon I kicked him repeatedly in the ribs and stomach. These kicks I now understand led directly to the death of Carl Walters shortly after I had effected my escape from the premises.'

'Death?' he repeated softly. 'You mean he's dead?'

'I mean you killed him. I have made this statement of my own free will and so on and so on. Get that typed out, Simpson, then bring it back for signature.'

Paul watched the sergeant leave the office with his solemnly copied shorthand notes. He smiled to himself. The style was wrong, Lou Kenzell didn't talk like that. But Kenzell was horrified. He was standing hypnotised as the sergeant left.

'I was at the pictures,' he said numbly, 'I told you. I wasn't anywhere near Mr Temple's place. I don't even know where he lives. I went to the Academy.'

'Alone?' Inspector Vosper asked wearily.

'That's right. Is there any objection to my going to the pictures by myself?'

Vosper shook his head. 'But unfortunately it doesn't provide you with a very good alibi.' It was clear from his manner that the interrogation was over. They were passing the time until Sergeant Simpson returned.

'When one is innocent,' Kenzell said with an attempt at simplicity, 'one doesn't need an alibi.'

Charlie Vosper laughed unkindly.

'I'll tell you, I went to the Academy at about one o'clock, and I left around three. I'd only been back home a few minutes when your cowboys arrived to arrest me.'

'What film did you see?' asked Paul.

'*Hamlet.*' He turned defiantly to Paul. 'Do you want me to tell you the plot?'

'That won't be necessary. Did you see the entire film?'

'No, I was only there for two hours. I couldn't possibly have seen the whole film, could I?'

'No,' Paul agreed, 'it's a very long film.'

Charlie Vosper perked up with a sudden look of intelligence. 'Oh, I remember that film. With Laurence Olivier and Jean Simmons, the one in glorious Technicolor.'

'Yes,' Kenzell said eagerly, 'that's the one.' Then he suspected the trap. 'Or at least, I'm not sure whether it's in Technicolor. But Laurence Olivier was in it—'

'Not sure?' Vosper demanded angrily. 'You saw the film an hour ago and you forget whether it's in colour? You squalid little man, you can't even think of a decent alibi, can you? You're a petty crook, a small bit killer. Sit there and shut up till the sergeant comes back!'

Kenzell cowered back in his chair and kept silent.

Vosper was going through the contents of Kenzell's wallet. He put the large pile of bank notes in one corner of his blotting-pad, stacked the club cards, driving licence and credit cards in another corner. 'Did you know that you haven't signed your driving licence?' he demanded. 'That's a legal offence.' There were no incriminating letters. A few photographs, one of which was obscene, another of which was highly moral and depicted his late wife, two more were of men involved in his professional life. Vosper grinned.

'Here's a photograph of you, Temple.'

'Taken from one of my dust jackets,' said Paul. 'It's a wonder he picked me out from the crowd, isn't it?'

Paul picked up the second photograph. It showed a man with a toothbrush moustache and close-cropped hair, pointed features and the dapper dress of someone probably small and finicky. 'Well well,' said Paul, 'this is interesting.'

'Who is it?' Vosper asked.

'A man called Duprez.'

'Duprez? You mean that Frenchman who was killed in the air crash?' Vosper took the photograph and glowered at it. 'His name was Rene Duprez, born in Orleans, 1932. That's what it says on the back.'

Sergeant Simpson tapped on the door as he entered with the statement typed in duplicate. He gave a copy to Kenzell and the original to Inspector Vosper.

'Ah, good. Read that through, Kenzell, and then sign it. Take your time, there's no hurry.'

Kenzell read it through as he was told and then signed the confession. Paul Temple signed as a witness with the sergeant.

Chapter Nine

'Paul, I've been thinking about this business. About the Curzon case. There's an awful lot I don't understand.'

He smiled. 'There's quite a lot I don't understand myself, darling.'

They had been driving for six hours and Steve was feeling bored. She preferred a small car for such long journeys, where you were aware of the ride and could feel some sense of adventure. The smooth and spacious Rolls could be tedious. She had been staring from the window at the desolate moorland since Malton, wondering whether to wave at the sheep or eat a box of After Eights.

'Yesterday lunchtime, for instance,' she said. 'Who telephoned Mrs Balfour?'

'Kenzell, of course. But Walters was already outside watching the flat. He knew that we were at the Savoy, and as soon as he saw Kate leave he assumed that the flat was empty. So he broke in.'

'To steal the notebook,' Steve murmured. 'I suppose those figures give the whereabouts of a hoard of diamonds?'

'I suppose so.' Paul turned right on to the coast road, increased his speed and overtook a holiday coach. 'From the

114

plane that crashed on the cliffs. Obviously the Frenchman Duprez used to bring them over in charter planes which were diverted over the Yorkshire coast. He used to drop the package to a waiting fishing-boat and all was well, until that night when the plane dropped too low. I imagine that was how the plane came to crash, don't you?'

'Oh yes, of course,' said Steve. 'And when the plane crashed Curzon was too slow off the mark. Somebody else found the diamonds first.'

'Well done. Yes, and I think that was Baxter. He was a relatively unimportant member of the gang, but as soon as he found the diamonds he decided to play for higher stakes. He hid the package, and then tried to contact Curzon.'

'Why should he want to do that?'

'I suppose he wanted a more important role, more money. It's my guess that Baxter didn't know the identity of Curzon. He would have dealt with the top man through an intermediary.'

Steve nodded. 'I can see why he wanted Tom Doyle to look after the boys. He knew he was playing a very dangerous game.'

'Exactly.'

They swept over the brow of the hill and along the deserted lane. The Forestry Commission forest stretched away to their right in neatly regulated lines. There was a car in the distance, parked by the entrance to an authorised Forestry Commission walk. A nature lover at large.

'So who is Curzon?' asked Steve.

'Well,' Paul said thoughtfully, 'it might be Lord Westerby, or Peter Malo, it might be Tom Doyle, even, or Dr Stuart . . .' He drove into the side of the lane and pulled up by the parked car. 'Having trouble, doctor?' he called.

It was Dr Stuart's battered Rover. The bonnet was up and Dr Stuart was staring perplexedly at the engine. He had prodded the parts he recognised and given the wheels an angry kick, but that had exhausted his mechanical resources. 'There's a gremlin in the water supply,' he said to Paul. 'Boiling like mad, and the engine has no power.'

Paul peered knowledgeably under the bonnet. 'Ah yes, I see what's wrong,' he said. 'There you are, a loose fan belt.'

'Incredible,' said the doctor. 'And now what happens?'

'Oh, we just wallop that bit there with something heavy and then tighten a nut.'

'Amazing.'

Paul belaboured the appropriate bit with a crowbar and then crawled underneath the car with an adjustable spanner. The doctor turned to Steve. 'I admire a man who knows how to strip down a car. The internal combustion engine is a complete mystery to me.'

'Paul knows about loose fan-belts,' Steve said unfairly. 'We had one a month ago and we spent three hours in a layby outside Oxford waiting for a man to come and mend it.'

A few moments later Paul emerged looking dirty but pleased with himself. 'There,' he said, 'that should have fixed it.' He leaned into the car and pressed the starter. The engine roared into life. 'You won't have any more trouble with that.'

'Extraordinary. I'm terribly grateful, Temple. I'd have missed my surgery if I'd had to walk from here.'

'Think nothing of it, doctor.' Paul wiped his hands on a clump of grass. 'By the way, I'm sorry about your friend. I feel in a way responsible as he died burgling my flat.'

'Which friend? Oh, you mean poor old Walters.' Dr Stuart switched off the ignition in his car and then sat conversationally on the running board. 'Yes, he was an engaging character.

Quite a rogue, I should think, but I became quite fond of him. You don't meet many people like him in Dulworth.'

Paul agreed. 'Had you known him long?'

'No, not really. I met him about six months ago. He came to the surgery one morning with a nasty gash on his hand. I did what I could for the laddie, and since it was lunchtime I let him take me down to The Feathers for a bite to eat. After that I suppose I saw him most times when he was up here.'

'Why did he come up here?' Paul asked.

'Business, I suppose, although he never discussed it with me. Apparently he ran a couple of clubs in London.' Dr Stuart smiled sadly. 'If he thought he could open up a gambling club in Yorkshire I'm not surprised he ran into trouble.' He shook his head sadly and climbed back into his car. 'I'll be seeing you two again, no doubt.'

'Almost certainly,' said Paul. He prepared to drive off, but as an afterthought he asked whether Diana Maxwell was better.

'Aye, she's back at home now, although I've confined her to bed for a week.' With a wave of his hand and a splutter of exhaust Dr Stuart bumped on to the road and drove away. Paul followed him across the moors as far as the Whitby road and then they parted company.

It was eight o'clock when they reached the hotel and tottered into their suite. 'Phew!' said Steve, 'I'm hot and jaded. I think I need a shower.' She hurried into the bathroom while Paul was taking the succession of messages that were waiting. She slipped out of the orange cotton dress and turned on the shower.

The water was cool and exhilarating. Steve waved her arms in the spray and absent-mindedly listened to Paul making his telephone calls. She heard him call Room Service for two long, iced drinks. It was, she decided, a blissful evening. A stray fly was buzzing against the window. The sound of summer. Voices in the distance of children playing on the beach.

'Hurry, Steve! Lord Westerby is expecting us at eight-thirty.'

But Paul was on the telephone again when she came out of the shower in her bath towel. Steve selected her Giselle dress with the ruched shoulders and bodice and the long sleeves falling to the ground in a point.

'I'm talking to Inspector Morgan,' Paul whispered with his hand over the receiver. 'He says that Tom Doyle is drinking like a fish and behaving strangely.'

Steve pursed her lips in polite surprise and half listened to the telephone conversation while she sipped her drink.

'So where do you think Tom's finding the money for this kind of living?' Paul asked the inspector. 'It sounds expensive.'

As Paul continued discussing the transformation Steve indicated her wristwatch. 'Half past eight,' she mouthed, 'dinner with Lord W.' She drained her glass and stood up in anticipation of leaving. The shower had completely revived her.

'I'm sorry, Inspector, I must go. My wife is waiting . . .'

Paul drove too fast out of the narrow streets of Whitby and then pressed down hard on the accelerator as they reached the moorland road. Steve closed her eyes. Tom Doyle was behaving strangely, she understood, but that was no reason for driving the Rolls into a ditch.

'I'd like to know where he's getting the money from,' Paul said at last. 'Inspector Morgan thinks someone is giving Tom Doyle money to stop him from talking, but I'm not so sure.'

'Lord Westerby?' asked Steve.

'I don't know.' Paul swerved with a screech of tyres round a sudden war memorial. 'Why does Lord Westerby crop up so often? Dammit, we have to work out some proof of Curzon's guilt, that's the only thing of importance. We don't need Tom Doyle to make things more complicated.'

'Do you mean,' Steve asked suspiciously, 'that you know who Curzon is?'

'Of course I know, that's the easy part. But proving—' He stamped on the brakes, swore angrily and sent the car into the side of the road. 'Did you see that? The bloody fool stepped in front of the car!'

Steve grinned. 'Darling, that's a telegraph pole. It didn't move.'

'Not that. The drunk in the ditch!'

The drunk turned out to be Tom Doyle, and instantly Paul's mood changed again. He accepted the stream of abuse with gravely apologetic good humour. 'I'm sorry, Tom,' he said, 'I didn't know it was you. Let me help you up.' He pulled the man out of the ditch and brushed some of the more obvious debris off his battered clothing.

'Didn't know it was me?' He swayed perilously. 'You mean you drive safely past your friends? Mad, that's what you are. I thought you'd gone back to London. They're all mad in London.' He took a hip flask from his pocket and drank from it. 'The roads aren't safe these days. You need a drink to pluck up courage to go home.'

'Get in, Tom, I'll drive you home.'

Paul pushed him in from behind while Steve leaned over and helped from the inside of the car. They eventually stretched Tom Doyle out across the back seat, where he lay muttering to himself about drivers driving him to drink. 'No wonder there's so much death on the road,' he said meaningfully.

Steve hunched herself against the door as Paul continued the journey. This was an evening of poise and immaculate turnout. She didn't want Paul's wretched friends or murder suspects breathing beer all over her. Or whisky. Whatever it was in the flask. She watched the moon over Fylingdales.

'What do you want to come back here for?' Doyle was muttering. 'Rotten hole. I'd get out myself if it wasn't for the easy money. Bloody dump. There's nothing in rotten Dulworth Bay except easy money. Lots of easy money, that's all.'

'He's drunk,' Steve said distastefully.

'Must be,' said Paul. 'I haven't noticed any easy money.'

'If you've got your head screwed on!' said Tom Doyle. He huddled in the corner and closed his eyes. 'Got to have your head screwed on and your eyes open,' he muttered. He lifted his feet on to the seat and appeared to fall asleep.

Paul had no idea where Tom Doyle lived, so when they reached Dulworth Bay he had to wake the man up and ask. It took a few moments and some vigorous shaking to revive him.

'Where am I?' he demanded blearily. 'What's all this about?'

'You're in Dulworth,' said Paul. 'I don't know your—'

'This'll do.' They were at the top of the main street running down to the sea. There was a pub opposite with peeling weatherboard, and the sounds of festivity had reached Doyle's consciousness. 'How much do I owe you?'

'We'll forget about that, Tom,' he said with a laugh.

'No we won't! I've got the bloody money and I'll pay.' He drew a handful of coins from his pocket. 'I know how expensive a taxi is to run.' He thrust a fifty pence piece into Paul's hand. 'There! Keep the change.' He tottered away to the pub muttering about extortion and the high cost of taxis.

Paul drove on. 'Do you want the window open, darling?' he asked.

'No, I don't think so.' She sighed. 'Something must be bothering poor Tom Doyle.'

Lord Westerby was a good and portly host. They were waiting for Peter Malo to return from his round of the estate – whatever that meant – before going in to dinner. But His Lordship's port was the best and he had provided Paul with an Havana cigar. He had complimented Steve on her dress, adding ungraciously that he had assumed she would be a man with a name like Steve.

'Don't approve of all these women called Bobbie and Billie and Arthur,' he barked at Paul. 'Girl my niece lived with was called Bobbie, and look what happened to her – somebody shot her.' With some ingenious logic Lord Westerby linked the girl's death with the fact that young men wear their hair long, then he padded across to the port for a refill.

'Just been reading your review of that book on crime,' he called gruffly. 'Don't usually read those intellectual weeklies, they're all pink if you ask me. But I liked your review. Damned amusing!' He was large and affable and slightly daunting.

'Thank you,' said Paul.

'Not sure that I agree with you about crime being caused by poverty. Crime's fun, isn't it? What about the way we behaved at Eton, eh? and in the officers' mess? We played hell with life and property for the sheer hell of it. Cocking a snoot at society, eh, Mrs Temple?'

'Yes,' she said. 'Paul has argued the same point in his more sober moments. He said that if it's money you're after the best thing to do is to get a job.'

'Crime doesn't pay, eh?' He glanced up at the portraits on the walls of eleven previous Lord Westerbys. They shared the plump expression of surprised pain which lurked around the present peer's eyes. 'So what is the motive for the mayhem up here in Dulworth? Money or fun?'

'Money,' said Paul, 'in the first place. Although fear has dominated our killer's activities since Bobbie Jameson was killed. The killer was terrified, for instance, that Miss Maxwell was going to talk, and he spent a lot of unnecessary energy preventing her.'

The door from the hall opened and Diana Maxwell came in looking wraithlike in her long brocade dressing-gown. She was pale and she moved slowly, but otherwise she was as striking as ever. Lord Westerby hurried across to take her arm and lead her to the sofa.

'Did I hear my name?' she asked.

'I was saying,' said Paul, 'that Curzon has devoted a lot of time to preventing you from talking to me. But it made no difference. I've completed the jigsaw puzzle without your help. The last piece fell into place as we were driving here tonight.'

Diana Maxwell looked apprehensively at her uncle. 'Do you mean, Mr Temple, that you know who Curzon is?'

'Not only that, Miss Maxwell, but tomorrow I'll prove it.'

'Oh dear.'

Steve leaned forward in her chair. 'What happened as we were driving here tonight, darling?'

'Something you said. It was a small, seemingly unimportant thing. You remember I asked you whether you wanted the window open?'

'I remember. What was so significant about that?'

'You said no.'

Steve stared in surprise. 'Good Lord. Yes. Yes, I see what you mean.' She turned pale as she realised the significance of Paul's point. 'But surely that doesn't mean—'

Lord Westerby slapped his glass on the tray. 'Damned if I know what you're all talking about, Temple. I never could do jigsaw puzzles. Shall we go and eat?' He took Diana Maxwell's arm. 'Can't wait all night for my secretary. He should have been back hours ago.'

At that moment Peter Malo returned, scratched and bruised from an argument with his car. 'It wouldn't start,' he said bitterly. 'I had to push it up the hill three times and it damned near ran me over. Hello, Temple. Mrs Temple. Sorry if you're starving on my account.'

Lord Westerby pottered about pouring the young man a sustaining whisky and enjoining him to change before dinner. 'Peter's helpless with a car,' he said, possibly as a joke. 'If it doesn't spring to life the moment he presses the starter he flies into an absolute panic.'

'It looks more as though the car panicked,' said Steve.

Diana Maxwell dabbed sympathetically at a trickle of blood on Peter Malo's face. 'You missed a nicely enigmatic conversation just now, Peter. Mr Temple has been explaining how he knows the identity of Curzon. He's going to prove it tomorrow.'

'I don't believe there is such a person,' Peter Malo said irritably. 'It's a lot of damned nonsense.'

'You'll see tomorrow.'

They went through to dinner. Lord Westerby kept the conversation on general topics, such as the youth of today and the British working man, on all of which he had a lot to say. Diana Maxwell was silent through the meal, and Peter Malo when he joined them simply acted as foil to his master's prejudices. Steve would have been extremely bored, except that the food was delicious and the waiter kept refilling her glass with wine.

By the brandy and coffee stages she had mellowed sufficiently to discuss the contemporary art scene with Peter Malo and find him interesting. They shared disparaging jokes about the minor masters collected by the ninth Lord Westerby for the baronial walls, and they found they both knew Giles Branson of the Branson Galleries. But from the corner of her eye she observed that Paul was chatting up the Maxwell girl. Ten minutes later her husband went arm in arm with the shameless hussy on to the terrace.

'I'm a grass widow,' Steve said with a sigh.

Peter Malo laughed. 'I believe there's a full moon out there tonight. Diana is terribly subject to lunar influence.' He poured more brandy and turned the conversation to Picasso.

Lord Westerby remained at the head of the table, staring silently into his empty glass. His ebullience had left him.

On the terrace Paul and Diana Maxwell stood in silence, sipping brandy and listening to the crickets somewhere out on the lawn. Eventually Paul spoke. 'You think Lord Westerby is Curzon, don't you?'

She nodded miserably.

'Supposing you start at the beginning, Miss Maxwell. Tell me why you telephoned that night and arranged to meet me at The Three Boars.' He sat on the balustrade with his back to the lawn and smiled gently. You did telephone me, didn't you?'

'Yes, I did,' she said almost inaudibly.

'Well?'

She sighed. 'Well, about three months ago I discovered that my uncle and Peter Malo and Mr Baxter were engaged in a diamond smuggling organisation. Of course, when I found out I went to my uncle and said it had got to stop. I even threatened to call the police.' She smiled wryly. 'He affected to be desperately frightened. He said that the leader of the organisation was a notorious criminal called Curzon, and Curzon was the type who would take

124

the law into his own hands by killing anybody who stood in his way.'

She paused and lit a cigarette. 'I suppose that was true enough. Then about six weeks after the conversation with my uncle a plane crashed along Dulworth cove. Did you know about that?'

Paul said that he did.

'There was a man on board called Rene Duprez bringing diamonds into the country. He looked after the Amsterdam end of the operation. After the crash both my uncle and Peter tried to find the consignment of diamonds, but apparently Mr Baxter had found them. Baxter had hidden the diamonds, made a note of the hiding-place and then contacted my uncle. There was really quite a scene about it.'

Paul laughed. 'I believe you.'

'The row with Baxter went on for several days and then, to my horror, the Baxter boys disappeared. I was convinced that my uncle was responsible and that he was the notorious Curzon. I went down to my flat in London and contacted you.'

'Why didn't you meet me?'

She shrugged. 'Because when I left the telephone box I bumped into Peter Malo. He'd been following me, of course. I took him back to the flat and we talked for a while. It was rather a strange conversation, rather unexpected.'

'He convinced you that Westerby had nothing to do with the Baxter boys and that he was not responsible for their disappearance?'

'Yes,' she said in surprise. 'When I realised he was telling the truth I let Bobbie go in my place to fob you off, and I went back to Dulworth Bay with Peter.'

Paul asked why it had been necessary to send Bobbie Jameson along as stand-in.

'Peter was afraid that if nobody turned up at the pub you'd become interested in the Baxter case and discover about Westerby and the Curzon organisation. He told Bobbie to supply you with false information and throw you off the scent.'

'So why was she murdered?'

'Because my uncle heard that I'd made an appointment to see you and he wanted to make sure that if I did meet you I shouldn't talk. Unfortunately he knew nothing about Peter's arrangement with Bobbie. It was an unnecessary murder.'

'And I suppose he set fire to the Baxter cottage?' said Paul.

'I suppose so. You and Mrs Temple were at the cottage looking after the boys. I suppose my uncle thought you'd be bound to find the notebook if you stayed long enough.'

'I didn't even know there was a notebook to find.'

There was a chill in the evening air now and Paul noticed that the girl was shivering. 'Let's go back inside,' he said. 'You aren't really better yet, are you?' He led her back into the drawing-room. 'I'm grateful to you,' he murmured, 'for taking me into your confidence. I wonder whether you could do me one more favour?'

'Yes?' she asked.

'I wonder if you could lend me the use of your yacht tomorrow? I want to give a cocktail party, and it occurred to me that on board your yacht might be the appropriate place.'

'Of course, Mr Temple.'

Lord Westerby was slumped in an armchair scarcely listening to the fashionable chatter about Picasso's erotic drawings. Diana Maxwell went and sat on the arm of the chair and ruffled his hair. 'You're such a fool,' she said to him, 'not at all cut out to be a notorious criminal.'

Paul beckoned to his wife. 'Let's go, darling. I'm dead tired and I've developed a headache. Let's go home.'

Chapter Ten

The holiday was nearly over, and Steve was looking forward to going home for some peace. She leaned over the rail of the yacht and watched the rowing boat pulling slowly across the bay. She had seen enough of her childhood haunts this past week to last her another twenty years. This cocktail party was her private farewell to the past.

It had been a busy day, meeting Inspector Vosper off the train from London, lunching at the police station with Inspector Morgan and then out for an afternoon on the cliffs. Paul had been pleased with the day, and Vosper had puffed lugubriously after them without complaining. Steve only regretted the fact that the crowning event, the party on board the *Windswept*, was likely to be such a mundane affair. Lord Westerby, Peter Malo, Diana Maxwell, Dr Stuart, Charlie Vosper – not the most amusing of people.

She could hear the strains of modern jazz floating up from the lounge, and a bark of laughter indicated that Lord Westerby was in party mood. A clink of glasses explained perhaps why. Steve sighed. The rowing-boat had come alongside with Tom Doyle at the oars carrying Dr Stuart.

'Ahoy there, Mrs Temple!' the doctor called happily.

Steve waved down. 'We'd nearly given you up!'

'Maternity case.' They were by the ladder and Dr Stuart lurched to his feet. 'The baby kept changing its mind.'

'Careful!' Tom Doyle snapped as his boat rocked. 'And that's twenty-five pence you owe me, don't forget.'

'Ah yes, of course.' Dr Stuart searched his pockets for change while Tom Doyle clung to the ladder. 'I'm sorry, Mrs Temple, but can you give this laddie twenty-five pence? I seem to be out of change.'

'I've never known you when you weren't,' Doyle muttered.

Steve chuckled as the doctor climbed up the ladder. She helped him aboard and held him steady on deck. 'You'd better come up as well, Mr Doyle!' she called. 'I'll get Mr Temple to pay you.'

The scene downstairs was less festive than she might have imagined. Charlie Vosper was sitting in a corner drinking a pint of beer ('No spirits, thank you, Temple, I never drink when I'm on duty.') Lord Westerby was standing in the centre of the lounge demanding to know what they were doing there.

'I always wonder that,' Diana Maxwell drawled, 'whenever I find myself at a cocktail party.'

Paul was bustling about serving drinks, introducing Charlie Vosper to everybody as the star of the show and telling Westerby to relax on his own boat. 'Why, hello, Tom. I didn't expect to see you.'

'Mr Doyle wants twenty-five pence,' said Steve. 'He brought the doctor out here.'

Paul took the fisherman by the shoulder and brought him into the group. 'You might as well have a drink while you're here. Will you have a cocktail, or do you prefer to drink beer with Inspector Vosper?'

Vosper had moved across to the door. 'That beer is too

precious on a warm evening to give to uninvited guests.' He laughed heavily.

Peter Malo yawned. 'We've been on this yacht for exactly three-quarters of an hour, Temple. You still haven't told us why we're here.'

Charlie Vosper coughed. 'I'm afraid Mr Temple has a weakness for parties, especially this kind of party. When he was mixed up in the Gregory case he had the nerve to invite all the possible suspects to his flat. There are three bullet holes in his mantelpiece—'

'What's all this about suspects?' snapped Westerby.

'Tonight,' Vosper continued, 'he's invited all the suspects in the Curzon case.' He beamed a welcome to each of the guests in turn.

'Do you mean that Curzon—?' Peter Malo began nervously.

'Yes, is here in this room.'

Tom Doyle looked about him in dismay. 'Here, just a minute,' he protested, 'don't count me in on this. I wasn't even invited! I'll just take my money—'

'You're very welcome to stay, Tom,' murmured Paul.

'Bugger that for a laugh, I'm going!' Tom Doyle left his glass on the tray and went quickly for the door. But it was locked. He spun round angrily. 'What's the idea, Temple? Why is the door locked?'

Paul smiled. 'Obviously it's either to prevent someone from getting in, or to stop someone getting out.'

For a full ten seconds Tom Doyle looked dangerously likely to panic, but then he returned to pick up his pint of beer and sat on the floor without speaking.

'Come on, Temple, for God's sake,' said Dr Stuart. He added a handsome measure of whisky to his drink. 'The suspense is killing me. Am I Curzon or am I in the clear?'

'It'll be me,' said Lord Westerby, 'so don't burst your ulcers. My faithful niece told him last night, didn't you, my precious?'

Paul held up his hand for silence. 'Miss Maxwell told me about the diamond smuggling, and the consignment which Duprez was carrying when the plane crashed. But that's where the story really begins, when Philip Baxter found the diamonds and contacted Lord Westerby.'

'And why did he contact me?' Lord Westerby asked ironically.

'Because he thought you were Curzon.'

'There you are. Don't worry, Dr Stuart, you're in the clear.' Lord Westerby snorted angrily. 'He'll produce the diamonds in a moment like a blasted conjurer, and claim they were hidden in my pocket. Come on, Temple, show us the diamonds!'

Paul took a chamois leather bag from his pocket and tossed it to Lord Westerby.

'Where did you find them?' Westerby asked in dismay.

'In the caves, close to where the plane came down. It was a simple matter to find them with the measurements in the notebook, but impossible otherwise, as poor John Draper learned.' Paul settled himself comfortably in an armchair and abandoned for the moment all pretence at a cocktail party. 'John Draper was probably the smartest person involved in this case, but then kids are always better informed than adults. When I asked him about Curzon the boy immediately linked the disappearance of his friends with a schoolboy legend about smugglers and the air crash. The legend was mainly fiction, but like most local gossip it was based on a grain of truth. Anyway John Draper was sufficiently concerned for his friends to do something about them. But he lost his way and nearly starved to death.'

Lord Westerby grunted. 'Hmph,' he said, 'you're quite right, Temple. What you've said about the diamond smuggling is true. I take full responsibility for myself and my secretary. Baxter was involved as well, and the bounder ran off with these. I admit I wanted them back pretty badly. But I'm not Curzon. I swear to you, Temple, I'm not Curzon!'

'Philip Baxter thought you were,' Paul said gently. 'He was so sure of it that he lived in fear of you. He even sent for Tom Doyle and asked him to look after his boys. That was when Tom Doyle went to the cottage and saw you there with Carl Walters.'

'That's a lie!' snapped Westerby.

Paul turned enquiringly to Tom Doyle. 'Is it a lie?'

'Of course not.'

Westerby's eyes bulged with suppressed rage. 'You mean to say that you saw me at the cottage talking to Baxter? What?'

'Yes,' Doyle muttered. 'Well, I did see you, so why should I say I didn't?'

Inspector Vosper picked up some papers from the table by the bar. 'If I remember these reports in sequence, Doyle, you made a statement to the effect that you saw Lord Westerby and Carl Walters at the cottage, but later you retracted it. When Mr Temple questioned you—'

'I changed my mind.'

Vosper replaced the papers and stared at Doyle in disbelief. 'Now why should you do that?'

'Because Lord Westerby made it worth my while. He gave me a hundred quid and told me that if I kept my trap shut he'd pay me a great deal more.' He turned aggressively to Paul Temple. 'Well, it was easy money, wasn't it? I had a hundred quid the day after I made the statement and another hundred a couple of days ago. That was when I saw you in the road, wasn't it?'

Lord Westerby had risen to his feet in horror. 'It's a lie!' he said fiercely, 'a damned lie! I never gave him a penny, and I never asked him to contradict his statement. For God's sake, I didn't even know that he'd made a statement! Surely you don't believe the little swine?'

'Of course I don't,' Paul said calmly.

Tom Doyle gaped.

'Doyle, you remember the night Baxter sent for you – the night you went to the cottage? In my opinion you didn't see anyone that night except Philip Baxter. Philip Baxter told you that he was frightened of someone and that he wanted you to look after the boys. Don't interrupt! In my opinion you knew that Baxter was a member of the Curzon organization and you suspected that he was under the impression Lord Westerby was Curzon. Later when you made your statement to the police you played up this impression in order to throw suspicion on to Westerby. Then you had an even better idea: you pretended to change your mind.'

Doyle shrugged his shoulders. 'Why did I do that, in your opinion?'

'Because you knew perfectly well that it would make us even more suspicious of Westerby. You started to throw money about, act drunk, and in general convey the impression you'd been bribed by Westerby.'

Lord Westerby spluttered in astonishment. 'I say, Temple, you're not suggesting that Doyle is mixed up in this business? I mean, dammit—'

'Yea, you must be crazy!' said Doyle. 'If I'd been involved do you think Baxter would have trusted me with his kids?'

'Not if he'd known,' said Paul. 'It never so much as entered Baxter's head that you were mixed up in the Curzon organisation. He certainly never dreamed for one moment that in trying to hide the boys from Lord Westerby he was actually handing them over to Curzon.'

The silence was broken by the splash of a soda siphon as Lord Westerby replenished his glass. 'Bless my soul,' he muttered to himself. 'Tom Doyle, eh? Bless my soul!' He knocked back his drink in one, then turned to Paul in defeat. 'I'll tell you one thing, Temple, which I hadn't realised: crime's very democratic.'

Tom Doyle suddenly laughed. 'You silly old buffer! I was clever, that was why you worked for me. You didn't have the brains to support that damned great museum you live in, and you expected me to tug my forelock when we passed in the street! You make me laugh, your lordship!' Tom Doyle had drawn a knife from his belt and he held it in front of him. It was the sort of thing best suited for killing sharks or prising barnacles off the bottom of a boat, slashing seaweed off nets. 'The first one to come near me gets this in his stomach!' said Doyle.

'It won't help you,' Paul said sadly. 'But don't worry, nobody proposes to come near you.'

Doyle pointed the knife at Inspector Vosper. 'Unlock that door,' he commanded. 'Come on, quick – quick – quick!'

Charlie Vosper was a phlegmatic man at the best of times. But he unlocked the door. 'There,' he said, 'now you can make your escape in that rowing-boat.' He went back and poured himself another pint of bitter.

'Actually,' said Doyle, 'I thought of taking this old tub. I've already had a practice run with Mr Temple. But this time I think Peter Malo can be my co-pilot.' He gestured to Malo. 'Come on, buddy boy. It's you and me again, the old firm.'

A smile flickered across Peter Malo's face and he followed Doyle from the lounge. A moment later the door was locked from the outside. They were all prisoners.

'Ah well,' said Paul, 'now that we've disposed of the unpleasant part of the evening let's proceed with the party. Dr Stuart, another splash of whisky. Lord Westerby, bring your glass over here.'

Steve was taken aback. 'But, darling, shouldn't we do something? I mean, he's escaping, isn't he?'

The yacht shuddered as the engines rumbled into life, there was a clanking sound as the anchor was raised, and then they were moving out into the North Sea.

'They'll have to stop some time,' said Paul, 'and when they do they'll be arrested. Inspector Vosper has his team waiting along the coast and they'll know what to do. The air waves are probably humming all over Europe already. So enjoy the cruise. This is just what Miss Maxwell needs to complete her convalescence, isn't it, Dr Stuart?'

'Aye,' said the doctor, 'and it's all on the National Health.' He chuckled idiotically at his joke until three blasts on the horn of a passing steamer attracted his attention. The passengers were waving happily at them and loud pop music proclaimed their pleasure.

Epilogue

Dulworth Bay was a peaceful place at night when the tide was out. The sea lapped gently at the sides of the yacht and the full moon glimmered in the waves. The distant lighthouse was the only sign of life. It was half past three; the party was over, but nobody felt like going home.

The *Windswept* had been boarded by police shortly after one o'clock and Doyle had been arrested following a brief but desperate battle. Peter Malo had been arrested without resistance. A coastguard had stayed on board to bring them home to Dulworth.

It hadn't been much of a party really, Steve decided. The Curzon case had been the only successful topic of conversation, and it had cropped up too often.

'I thought you were going to prove that Curzon was me,' said Dr Stuart. 'I was quite disappointed when you picked on poor Tom Doyle.'

'I'm sorry,' said Paul. 'But once we accepted Doyle's story about the boys it had to be pure coincidence that you were in the lane that afternoon.'

'Aye, but it was a funny story. After all, when Doyle, or Curzon, had the boys why didn't he simply threaten

Baxter and demand the diamonds?'

'Because Doyle didn't know that Baxter had the diamonds. When Baxter found the diamonds he contacted Lord Westerby, and that was when people began to get hurt. Doyle knew very little about it.'

'So who murdered Baxter?'

'Peter Malo, I'm afraid. That was something which confused me for a long time. I thought it had to be Curzon who was running wild and hiring Lou Kenzell to retrieve the notebook. But in fact that was Peter Malo. He's a ruthless young man.'

Conversation had flagged after the arrests. Paul and Steve had gone up on deck to watch the stars. Dr Stuart had become rather drunk and he would keep humming Loch Lomond. They found Inspector Vosper standing on the bridge with the coastguard. He was still on duty.

'Let's go and sit on the prow,' Steve murmured.

When the yacht came into harbour Charlie Vosper went below to fetch Lord Westerby. The hereditary earl was glassy eyed and unsteady on his feet but he still retained a bluff dignity. 'I say, Temple,' he called. He left Charlie Vosper waiting on the gangplank. 'Temple, I've been worried all blasted evening. I mean, dammit, you've been telling every-body about our smuggling ring and all the rest of it, but you haven't told me the only thing I want to know.'

'What's that?' Paul asked politely.

'Well, dammit, what was all that about opening the window?'

Paul laughed. 'Yes, I'm sorry, that was a little cryptic. But it was the decisive point at which I realised that Doyle was the undoubted villain. He had been over-acting.'

'We gave Doyle a lift in the car,' Steve explained. 'He was supposed to be wildly drunk, just to prove that he had all the money you were giving him as a bribe. But he wasn't drunk at all. There was absolutely no smell of drink on the man.

'My wife,' Paul explained, 'is not too keen on the smell of alcohol. But when Doyle got out of the car she did not need the window open. That was all. Quite simple, really.'

'Bless my soul.' Lord Westerby turned in bewilderment to Inspector Vosper. 'I say, sergeant! Where are you?' He wandered off to the gangplank. 'All right, lead away.'

Steve sighed. 'Well,' she said, 'I suppose that's about it. Another Paul Temple crime solved. It's all over bar our holiday?' She leaned her head against his shoulder and stared out across the bay. 'Isn't it a beautiful night? So quiet and still, so warm.'

Paul put his arm round her and closed his eyes.

'We're alone now,' said Steve. 'There's only Diana Maxwell down in her bunk asleep, and old Dr Stuart in a drunken coma. Don't you find the sea romantic?'

'Well, yes,' he began.

'Let's have another drink to cheer ourselves up. And then we can bathe in the moonlight. Do you know, we've never bathed in the moonlight together?'

Paul yawned. 'Darling, it's nearly four o'clock. I'm tired. You were dozing off yourself just now—'

'Now listen to me, Paul Temple, you're going into that water or I'll damn well throw you overboard! Take your choice!'

She had spoken rather loudly and somewhere beyond the harbour a dog barked. A few moments later there was a splash, and somebody cried for help. But it was late and nobody came to investigate. The dog seemed to have gone back to sleep.